on the Great Land

a novel
by
Emily Bieniek

D0967984

WARD STREET PRESS · SEATTLE · 2017

On the Great Land
Copyright © 2017 by Emily Bieniek.
All rights reserved.

No part of this publication may be reproduced or transmitted in any form or by any means without written permission from the publisher. Requests for permission to make copies of any part of the work should be emailed to the following address: info@wardstreetpress.com

If not available at your local bookstore, this book may be ordered directly from the publisher. For additional information about this book and about Ward Street Press, visit our web site at:

http://www.wardstreetpress.com

This book is a work of fiction. All characters, incidents, and dialogue are drawn from the author's imagination and are not to be construed as real. There is no portion of Anvil Mountain or the surrounding range where the wind will catch someone who jumps or falls off the edge of the mountain; this scenario was imagined for the purposes of the fictional story "Anvil Tavern."

Warning: This book contains themes of and references to abuse and self-harm that may be triggering.

On the Great Land
ISBN: 978-0-9887417-7-5

EDITORIAL CONSULTANT: SUSAN TOWLE
AUTHOR PHOTO: DAVID DODMAN
BOOK & COVER DESIGN BY VEE SAWYER

on the great land

TO MY PARENTS

contents

alaska maps

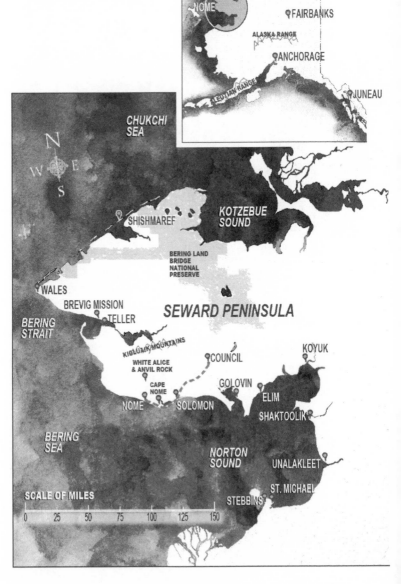

glossary

AAKA ■ Mother (Inupiaq).

AANII ■ Hello (Ojibwe).

AAPA ■ Father (Inupiaq). Can also be used to mean grandfather or stepfather.

AGUTAK ■ A traditional dessert, also known as *akutaq*, made with berries, greens and fish mixed with whipped fat, oil, or Crisco (Yup'ik).

ARCTIC ENTRY ■ A small room between the front door of the house and the door that leads to the inside of the house. Designed to prevent heat loss, people typically store outdoor gear in these spaces. Also called an arctic entryway (English).

ASIAVIK ■ Alpine blueberry (Inupiaq).

ATCHAAQLUK ■ Beach greens (Inupiaq).

BALACLAVA ■ Cloth headgear that covers the wearer's head, nose, mouth, and neck (English).

BUNSO ■ Youngest sibling (Tagalog).

KAUK ■ Walrus skin that is prepared as food (Inupiaq).

KAWERAK, INC. ■ A non-profit organization organized by the Bering Straits Native Association after the passage of the Alaska Native Claims Settlement Act that provides a variety of services to residents in the Bering Straits region.

KIMAGLUK ■ Edible green; half-cooked greens (Inupiaq).

MITKOTAILYAQ ■ Tern (Inupiaq).

MUKLUKS ■ Boots, traditionally made of reindeer, caribou, or sealskin (Yup'ik). *Kamiks* in Inupiaq.

NEEZHODAY ▪ Twin (Ojibwe).

NIAQUQ ▪ Head or cranium (Inupiaq).

NIQIPIAQ ▪ Traditional food; Inupiaq food (Inupiaq).

OOGRUK ▪ Bearded seal (Inupiaq). Can also be spelled as *ugruk*.

SITNASUAK NATIVE CORPORATION ▪ A corporation created under the Alaska Native Claims Settlement Act with headquarters in Nome, Alaska.

TUKAIYUK ▪ Beach green; sea lovage (Inupiaq).

ULU ▪ A smooth, rounded knife (Inupiaq).

UQSRUQ ▪ Oil; seal oil (Inupiaq). Can also mean blubber and can be spelled *uksruk*.

on the great land

introduction

To a casual observer, the Kigluaik Mountains, a low range situated just south of the Arctic Circle, exemplify the pristine ideal of the unexplored Alaskan wilderness. Dappled, treeless tundra undulates across the Kigluaik slopes, offering berries and greens in the perpetual sunlight of the summer months and surrendering to deep drifts of snow in the dark winter. Moose, foxes, bears, caribou, ptarmigans, and muskoxen roam freely on this arctic desert, supported by a thick floor of permafrost; radiantly-plumed birds lay their eggs in the spring growth on the tundra every year, then fly south again with their young as the nights grow longer.

The Kigluaik Mountains, however, are not untouched; Inupiaq and Yup'ik people have lived on and at the edges of the range for generations, hunting, fishing, and camping in the dry, cool region. A closer study of the foothills, too, reveals the industrial ruins of a century of European settlement: rusted train tracks, collapsed aqueducts, and abandoned dredges litter the landscape, overgrown by minute creeping plants and barnacle roots.

The small town of Nome rests in an outer cradle of the Kigluaik foothills, on the coast of the Bering Sea. Legend has it that three Swedish men found gold in those hills at the end of the nineteenth century, set up camp on Inupiaq and Yup'ik territory, and called that camp Nome. When news spread of gold on the boreal coast, the miners, prostitutes, priests, and government agents who had arrived late to the California Gold Rush changed their course and headed north, and all their sins and hopes followed them to Nome as they stirred up the last dregs of Manifest Destiny. Within a few years, Nome's population swelled from a humble mining camp to a city of thousands. As Nome grew, the settlers set their sights on the mountain range interior, dreaming of further expansion. They imported wood and copper and attempted to manage the land with infrastructure, but they were unprepared for the series of plagues that soon befell the town: fires, storms, and illnesses drove many people south again.

Now, Nome serves as a hub for the Inupiaq, Central Yup'ik, and Saint Lawrence Island Yup'ik villages in the Bering Straits region, from Stebbins in the South to Shishmaref in the North. Accessible only by boat, plane, and dogsled, Nome's population fluctuates in the sunlit months as Iditarod mushers race their dog teams to the Burled Arch on Front Street and young men across America succumb to the call of the rumor-fueled gold rush under the Bering Sea. Nome's four thousand permanent residents, meanwhile, form a quiet community in the arctic. They live abreast of the industrial ruins, leaving them intact to serve both as reminders of the vain ambitions of the town's early colonial era and as testaments that they, too, are transient dwellers on the great land.

the beginning

THE SUN PEERED OVER THE BERING SEA, casting a deep amber glow on the violet streets of Nome and lacquering each snow-covered rooftop in gold. On the far northern edge of town, rosy shadows bloomed through the floor-to-ceiling windows of the Norton Sound Regional Hospital as the sun began its quick ascent. The radiant sunrise masked the lateness of the day: because of the cant of the earth, this first flash of light heralded noon.

Lynn paused with her seven-year-old patient and her patient's mother on the third floor of the hospital, resisting the instinct to shield her eyes against the light. "Are you sure you need to leave?" she asked the mother. Lynn's patient bounced anxiously on her toes and turned her back to the window. The little girl's hair was tangled, and she had dark circles under her eyes. "We have staff here who can talk to your daughter now, even just to see how she's feeling."

"We're okay," the mother said, looking down. "Should be getting her some lunch."

Lynn tilted her head to get her eyes out of the mid-winter sun. "We have lunch here. You can both eat in the cafeteria, my treat. I really recommend that your daughter see someone as soon as possible. It'll be completely confidential." Lynn paused. "Would you like to talk to someone as well?"

"Gotta be getting back," her patient's mother said softly.

"Okay, well, let's get you both back here for a follow-up soon. Does Thursday at nine work?"

The mother shrugged.

"Great," Lynn said. "I'll get that in at the front desk. See you then."

Lynn watched the pair reach the elevator bank, then leaned her forehead against one of the hallway windows. Across the dirt-packed highway, Nome's streets led south into the sturdy ice of the Bering Sea, where gold miners had pitched and tented their winter dredges alongside strings of local crab pots. Snow machines, cars, and trucks sunk into almost every front yard in town, wheels crystallized in the snow. Beyond the last row of houses at the western edge of Nome, Lynn could make out the Coast Guard helicopter hangar and county jail. The airport was out that way too, toward the port, although she couldn't see it. On her left, the easternmost run of Front Street, the main drag, turned into a state highway that ran next to the beach, across the open tundra, and into the sun-drenched foothills that circled the cape toward Council, one of the few communities accessible from Nome by road. A herd of silver-backed muskoxen lay settled in the groove of the northern highway embankment, almost still enough to be mistaken for snowdrifts. The only movements in the mid-day sunrise came from the ravens that jostled each other for space on the telephone wires that connected Nome with the rest of the world.

Lynn straightened, leaving patches of fog and sweat on the window glass. The hallway was empty, but she didn't want any patients to see how tired she was. She glanced down at her cell phone. No new messages, no missed calls. Lynn sighed. She needed to talk to her brother about her recent cases. Her seven-year-old patient had told Lynn during her annual physical that she was from one of the Native villages and had moved to Nome after her uncle had grabbed her under her nightie. Earlier in the week, a teenager whose spine had cracked under the wheels of a drunk driver was pronounced dead on arrival. Another girl, only twelve years old, had been medevaced into Nome after trying to slit her wrists. Nursing school in suburban Minneapolis hadn't prepared Lynn for such concentrated sadness. Her twin brother, Wade, was living with their parents while studying to be a therapist, and she needed his calm, efficient wisdom. When they were little, her mother used to call them both *neezhoday*, twin in her Ojibwe language, so often that Lynn thought she and Wade shared it as their given name. Now her brother,

her second heart, was silent. She hadn't blamed him at first — she had been the one to assert her independence by moving to Alaska — but now the deep hollow his heart had left in her chest was filling with the sadness of the long, subarctic winter nights in the emergency ward. She wished that she had listened to him when he had asked her not to take a job so far away from home.

Outside, the sun paled as it reached its full winter height, its bottom edge hovering just above the frozen sea. When Lynn had arrived in Nome in the early fall, when the tundra displayed lush reds, golds, and browns, everyone she met — Norton Sound Regional Hospital workers, gold miners, KNOM Radio DJs, Sitnasuak Corporation employees, Kawerak nonprofit workers, Coast Guard pilots, even transient seasonal visitors — told her, as the days approached twenty-one hours of darkness, it was essential to maintain a routine: to wake up in the morning no matter the sun's schedule, to eat three meals a day, to take vitamins, to go outside, to exercise, and to go to bed well after the afternoon sunset. Lynn had tried to take their advice, these kind people who wanted to welcome her to their arctic home, but the winter darkness left her perpetually dazed, as if she had just woken up from an overlong dream.

❖ ❖ ❖

AN AMBER BEAM OF LIGHT STREAKED THROUGH THE DARK dawn and shattered against the frost that spiderwebbed across the inside of Lynn's bedroom window. Lynn opened one eye to watch the sunrise brighten the winter sky to gold. She stretched out on her twin bed and looked at the travel clock on her nightstand. It was fifteen minutes past twelve. She had slept through her weekend alarm. It would be dusk in less than two hours.

Even the birds were silent this morning. The skating rink on the next block was empty. Lynn could only see a narrow sliver of Front Street from her window, but she didn't see anyone walking to the Post Office or the bars. Lynn closed her eyes and opened them again slowly; now that the day was halfway over, she didn't feel any urgency to get out of bed. She still had nearly seven hours until she had to be at the hospital for her rotational weekend shift. When the sun had cleared the horizon, Lynn tried some experimental stretches before throwing back her sheets.

Lynn slid her bare feet into the slippers next to her bed, not bothering to fully dress before turning her face to the window. It was important to absorb as much sunlight as she could, and she wasn't going to venture out into the subzero weather until she absolutely had to. The walls of the apartment complex were a foot thick to prevent heat loss, so Lynn had to lean into the window until she was seated on the sill to get any sun on her face. She checked her phone. No new messages during the night.

From her second-floor vantage point, Lynn could see that the family in the house directly across the street from her apartment complex was sitting together at their kitchen table. Lynn let herself reminisce about the Greek yogurt and blackberries that her mother served with breakfast every weekend as she shook a gummy vitamin from the container next to her bed and chewed. It looked like the family below was eating cereal.

A small moan in the next room shattered her reverie. Lynn shook her head. The apartment complex Lynn shared with the other hospital workers was as quiet as the town below, which only amplified Brian and Suze's faint shifting in the room next to hers. Lynn was sure that Suze was about to tell her about their affair, but for now Lynn would let them think that they were being quiet enough. She tried not to listen and leaned further into the sill to see what other families were eating for breakfast.

Lynn's new angle let her peer into the houses adjacent to her apartment complex. From here, she could see a man's hand resting on the back of the empty chair next to him as he sat at his kitchen table. Everything about that arm, Lynn thought, looked cozy: the strong fingers, the protective way the forearm rested on the back of the chair, the thick, gray Carhartt work shirt pushed just past the wrist. Lynn rested her forehead between the mandalas of frost on the window and considered going back to bed.

Someone must have pointed, Lynn thought later, because suddenly the man looked over his shoulder and through the kitchen window. Following an unseen cue, he flicked his eyes up at Lynn. She recognized him as someone she passed in the street all the time, a young man with a handsome face and slight mustache, usually trailed by a jumpy black and white mutt that sniffed around his ankles. They stared at each other for a moment. Then Lynn remembered that she was only wearing a white t-shirt, probably see-through in the now-brilliant sunlight, and ducked. I should have just waved, she thought, as she wedged her shoulders awkwardly between the bed and dresser. She grabbed her bathrobe off the floor, crossed it over her chest, and stood. When she looked at the window again, the man had turned away.

Lynn shook her head and pulled on the pair of thick leggings that lay crumpled on the floor next to her bed. She padded past the parallel rows of closed bedroom doors on her floor and down the stairs to the apartment common area. The large room stretched the entire length of the complex and included a kitchen with an island, a dining room table that seated eight, and four mismatched brown couches and two rocking chairs stationed around a small TV set. The kitchen, living, and dining areas had been painted contrasting shades of beige to differentiate the spaces, but a navy wall-to-wall carpet dominated the room, creating the impression that everything in the common area was blue. Things that people had left behind over the years covered the space: mismatched throw pillows, picture frames full of smiling strangers, empty handmade flower pots. A harpoon made of wood and walrus ivory was mounted above the door of the complex. Bottles lined the tops of the high kitchen cabinets, collecting dust.

Lynn took down the thick gray blanket that insulated the window between the kitchen and the living room to let in the pale afternoon sunlight. An empty bottle of wine and two glasses perched on the kitchen island, and a blanket was thrown casually over one of the couches. Lynn straightened the blanket and cushions, put the wine glasses in the dishwasher, and wiped down the kitchen island and dining room table before starting a pot of coffee. She settled onto one of the couches and pulled out her phone, somewhat guiltily streaming on the house's limited Wi-Fi allotment for the month. She didn't feel too bad about it, though; if Brian and Suze could sleep together without telling the rest of their flatmates, then surely Lynn was allowed to use a little extra Internet.

A loud knock on the door made Lynn jump. She crossed her arms over her chest and hopped through the arctic entry. Standing among the discarded parkas and boots in the small room, she shook her head quickly and stretched her mouth into a tight, toothy grin to warm up her face. She closed the inside door to the arctic entry and opened the front door. Ethan, one of the young men in town who joked with Lynn and her endless rotation of housemates at the bars on Front Street, stood shyly on the front porch. Snow stuck to his goatee and eyebrows, prematurely aging him.

"Hey," he said, his voice shivering. "Fucking freezing." He held out a pair of heavy gray-brown crabs and Lynn took them instinctively by their dangling legs. Ethan buried his hands in the pockets of his work coat and continued, "Checked the pots today. These aren't regulation size — can't sell them. Perfectly good to eat, though — thought you ladies and Brian could use some grub. Jesus, weather's so fucked up this season. Sorry, can't stay — not dressed warm enough. Get back inside!"

"Thanks, Ethan!" Lynn said. Ethan smiled sweetly and bounded away down the front steps, hampered only a little by his heavy waterproof gear. The snow on the porches and doorframes along the road glowed lavender in the subarctic afternoon, and Lynn paused to admire the light before shutting the door with her hip.

Inside, Lynn held up the two crabs to examine them: they were just over half the size of the crabs that she, Suze, and Brian had bought for themselves at Norton Sound Seafood Products last month, but she trusted Ethan that they were edible. The crabs waved their front claws helplessly, stunned by the cold but already beginning to thaw into action in the warm house. The crabs from last month had been easy for the three housemates to kill and steam, so Lynn decided to handle this smaller pair on her own. She put both animals on the table, so she could prepare the kitchen while they were still too weak to skitter away. They lay on their backs, exposing mottled yellow underbellies. Lynn filled the biggest pot in the kitchen with water and set it on the stove to boil, then pulled on a pair of oven mitts to protect her hands from the crabs' prickly shells.

One of the crabs was getting close to flipping itself upright, so Lynn picked up one crab in each hand, threw the larger one in the freezer, and took the other to the sink. With a quick twist, Lynn cleanly separated the twin halves of the crab's shell. A geyser of seawater erupted from the crab's body, spilling a salty odor into the kitchen. The crab Lynn had killed last month had been large and active, but at least its shell had been brittle; this smaller crab was suppler, and she had to twist each limb several times before she could tear it away from the crab's abdomen. She finished the first crab in disgust and shuddered as she started the second. By the time all twelve brown and yellow legs were in the pot, Lynn felt nauseous and exhausted. She tossed the crab bodies into the trash before sitting down on one of the kitchen island stools to check her phone.

Brian wandered downstairs, stretching in his hoodie and pajama pants. "Oh hello, favorite wife!" he exclaimed, suddenly animated upon seeing Lynn.

"Hey there, honey!" Lynn squealed back. With nine girls and Brian in the housing unit this rotation, the sister-wives jokes flew early and often in the common area. "I made you some coffee!"

"Just for me?" Brian pulled Lynn into an affectionate noogie, then glanced over at the stovetop. "What's that?"

"Ethan dropped off some crab!"

"And you answered like that? He must have been delighted."

"Shush, you."

Brian let Lynn go to look in the pot. "These are done," he said, and turned off the burner. The crab legs glowed scalding red beneath the water, and Brian reached in to test their texture with a fork. "You didn't steam them? I guess they're pretty small. Are we going to get salmonella? Should I make them into crab cakes for dinner? Man, we haven't had any meat in a while. This is great. Reminds me that I gotta call Dave to see if he's got anything left over."

"Whatever you say, dear. Is the coffee done? Can you pour me a cup?" Lynn shook out Friday's *Nome Nugget* newspaper with a flourish and tried to swing her short black hair over one shoulder. She sighed in frustration. She was trying to be frugal while living in Nome, but she should never have let Suze cut her hair; although her friend insisted her new bob was modern and flattering, Lynn missed her heavy tresses. She noticed, too, that Suze's hair remained long and auburn.

One of the younger rotational nurses stumbled downstairs, already dressed in pink running tights and gym shoes. She ran to the arctic entry without looking at Brian or Lynn.

"You know she leaves her shoes under the sink in our bathroom?" Brian said once they heard the front door slam shut. "It's so weird."

Lynn shrugged. She wondered what Brian said about her when she wasn't in the room.

Brian poured Lynn a cup of coffee as Suze descended into the kitchen, her prima ballerina composure in place. Brian didn't look at her as she announced, "Good afternoon!" to the room, and her expression deflated for a moment. Then: "What's that smell?"

"Crabs," Lynn said. "Ethan dropped them off."

"What a sweetheart! We talked about it at Breakers last night, but I didn't think he'd actually do it! People never remember promises they make at the bar."

Brian frowned into his coffee.

"Also, did you know that he's married? And has a kid? He's just like, a really sweet guy."

Lynn cleared her throat. "Brian's gonna fry them to make sure we don't get food poisoning."

"Crab tempura? I'm so excited!"

"Crab tempura? Jesus." Brian gaped at her. "Crab cakes," he said. "I'm making crab cakes."

"Whatever." Suze pulled her hair up into a bun, then drained the coffee pot and didn't start another one. "When do you guys have to go in today?"

"I have the day off," Brian offered. Suze tried to look surprised.

"I have to go in at seven," Lynn interjected. "Can we have dinner before then?"

"Of course!" Suze and Brian said in unison. Brian glanced sidelong at Suze, who did not return his look. Lynn shook her head and turned back to the *Nome Nugget*.

The three of them drank their coffee in silence, and Brian put on another pot. A pair of Icelandic physicians' assistants with rhyming names skipped downstairs with matching skis propped on their shoulders. Suze and Lynn waved as the girls headed out the door. "Anita and Benita?" Brian yawned once they were safely down the block. "Elsa and Helga? Magda and Agda?"

"I think it's Alida and Alfrida," Suze giggled. "I'm not kidding."

Brian and Suze drifted toward the television in the living room, and Lynn made sure the bowl of crab legs was safely hidden at the back of the refrigerator before joining them on one of the overstuffed couches. Of all their flatmates, Lynn, Brian, and Suze had been in Nome the longest, and while the newer staff embraced the novelty of winter activities like snowboarding and cross-country skiing, Lynn found that her days were getting quieter and quieter. Suze put on *Mixology*, which no one but Suze liked, and pulled a book onto her lap.

After half an episode, Lynn announced, "Well, I'm going to go call my family," and skipped through the kitchen and up the back stairs, ignoring the rustle that Brian and Suze created as they moved closer together behind her.

On their first day of their rotations, the orientation leader had stressed the importance of building a family together in Nome. The winter was long, he had said, and you needed to know that the people in your program were there to support you no matter what. For the first few months, Lynn, Brian, and Suze had taken the orientation leader's advice; they were a unit, the core group in a house that was constantly changing around them. Lynn knew Brian and Suze thought they were supporting her by pretending that their relationship hadn't changed since the first day they'd moved in together, but the secrecy shrunk the core group to two rather than keeping her inside their arctic family. I should just go home, she thought, but with Wade not speaking to her, she didn't know what home would be like either.

Every door in the long hallway upstairs was still closed. Lynn wondered where the rest of her flatmates were.

Lynn closed the door to her room and flopped down on her bed. Her room was plain, and, besides the bed and dresser, furnished only with a light wooden furniture set that included a desk, a chair, and a nightstand. Dull, stain-resistant carpeting covered the floor. Lynn had tacked photos of her family and friends over the tack holes left by previous tenants.

Lynn turned off the overhead fluorescent light and breathed in the deepening sunset. She saw that the window across the street, empty now, displayed traces of a gray carpet and a wooden table that matched her bedroom furniture. The sets might have been shipped up together on the same barge.

Her phone beeped. "*Aanii*! Love you!" the message from her mom read. "Making chili for dinner. Wade says hi!"

Lynn stared at the ceiling.

Lynn wondered how the year had degenerated so rapidly. She had looked forward to her new adventure in Alaska for months, her first time leaving home. Her arrival in August had been autumn-hued and lively. She had been excited to see Inupiaq and Yup'ik culture integrated into the town as soon as she stepped off the plane, and had even collected her bags next to the Nome public school cross-country team decked in sweatshirts that read "Nanooks" alongside a fierce polar bear graphic. But she had been embarrassed to admit to people in town that she had never visited her relatives who still lived on Ojibwe land, and it had taken her the rest of the daylight season to learn that going to the bars on Front Street in the sunlit summer nights left her too tired to explore the hilly tundra the next day. Her favorite place in town, she discovered, was the Quyanna Care Center, where she could sit with Alaska Native elders and listen to their stories about Nome in the old days or their homes in the villages that surrounded the town.

Then, in November, as the winter fog rolled over the mountains on the cape, Lynn had felt her mind dim. She suddenly found no joy in playing house with Brian and Suze, in hiking and exploring, in learning about Inupiaq and Yup'ik cultures, or even in the conversations she had in the Care Center. She had to consciously stretch her own face, which had settled into a permanent scowl, into different expressions whenever she wanted to talk to someone. On her better days, Lynn feared her new doldrums, but overall she had acclimated to her indifference with startling ease. She didn't know if this was how everyone felt during their first winter in the far north and didn't feel like she had anyone to ask. She tried so hard to be as cheerful around Brian and Suze as she had been when she first arrived in Nome. Now, she was afraid they hadn't noticed the change and wouldn't take her seriously if she talked to them about it. Besides, maintaining the illusion of normalcy did actually help Lynn feel better sometimes.

Lynn checked her cell phone again, almost physically feeling her twin's silence reject her across three time zones. She wanted to return to her old self before she went home, but her memories of how she used to act seemed hazy and inaccessible. She could not recapture the glee she knew she had felt when she had goofed around at her restaurant job or drove her car down the highway or teased her twin brother. She had to recover a little bit before going back; she did not want her parents to know that her only adventure away from Minnesota had been so difficult.

The sky flashed a blue-hued red, and the pitch-black night returned. Lynn lay blankly in the darkness.

Brian and Suze had reached a quiet equilibrium by the time Lynn reappeared in the kitchen. Suze sat on a stool and rested her book against the kitchen island while Brian, obviously having refused her help, prepared crab cakes and rice. Lynn felt the corners of her mouth turn downward. She shook her head and stretched her lips to grimace, then softened her features into a smile as her choppy hair came to rest around her face. "Looks wonderful!" she exclaimed, and Brian glanced at her appreciatively.

"How's your family?" Suze asked, looking up from her book.

"Great! I'm super hungry." Lynn began to chop some carrots to sauté. Suze was the nutritionist, so they had all agreed at the beginning of their rotation that cooking and meal planning should be her role in the house, but Suze had already started reading again. "Did those Icelandic girls come back?" Lynn asked.

"Yeah. They put on some really ugly sweaters and went back out without speaking to any of us," Brian said.

"I wonder if they're doing something fun that we weren't invited to," Suze said. She pulled her hair, which had fallen back around her shoulders in waves, into a Balanchine knot. "Like maybe a Christmas party."

"It can't be that fun. Maybe we were invited, but they didn't tell us."

"Yeah. Probably not, though. I feel like if there was something going on, Lynn would have been invited at least."

"You guys," Lynn protested. Brian and Suze smiled affectionately at her.

"Sorry this is late," Brian said, gesturing to the crab cakes frying on the stove. "I know you have to go soon."

Lynn shook her head. She pulled some tea lights out of one of the kitchen drawers, lit them, and set them on the large wooden table. Brian piled seven small crab cakes onto a plate, set it on the table, then brought over three plates, the bowl of rice, and sautéed carrots. He pulled up a chair next to Lynn. Suze got the silverware and sat across from Brian. She took the first crab cake.

"How is it?" Brian asked anxiously.

"You should start a cooking show," Suze teased.

"Remember when that camera crew followed us around for a week and decided we were too boring for a reality show?" Lynn asked.

"And look at us now," Suze said.

"You've gone through what, four boyfriends since then?" Brian asked.

"Shut up," Suze said. "At least I still have all my teeth."

"I look like a real Alaskan man now," Brian said, running his tongue over his chipped front tooth. The table fell silent as they all remembered rushing Brian to the hospital with a mouth full of blood after he'd fallen against a spike of ice while trying to scale the frozen Dorothy Falls waterfall.

Suze recovered first. "You should cook, like, walrus blubber," she said.

Brian shook his head. "I don't think you cook that," he said. "I'm pretty sure you only cook *kauk*. The skin. I think you eat the blubber raw. That's what we did up in Teller, I think, when we went to the dance festival."

"I know," Suze said. "I was there." She rolled her eyes and glanced at the clock. "Wait, Lynn," she said, "don't you have to go?"

"Shit!" Lynn stuffed the rest of her crab cake and as much rice as she could into her mouth. She threw her plate in the sink, jogged to the arctic entryway, and began pulling on her layers: the scrubs over her leggings and two pairs of socks, then snow pants and a parka, and finally her Sorel boots, balaclava, and gloves.

"See you!" Suze called before Lynn closed the living room door.

The cold bit savagely at Lynn's face as she stepped onto the porch. She bent her head almost to her waist and breathed hard into the balaclava, shoving her gloved hands into her pockets. The wind seeped through the shell of her parka and coiled tightly around her arms. Lynn had wondered more than once that winter, as she shuffled past the rows of single-story houses to the outskirts of town, if she would survive the short walk to the hospital.

A truck skidded around the next corner, and Lynn leapt onto the nearest stoop to get out of its way; on the back residential streets, two ATVs could pass each other easily, two cars could pass each other tightly, but a truck took up the entire road.

Lynn hopped off the porch and skated along the ice in the middle of the street toward the hospital, which glowed comfortably against the absolute blackness of the tundra on the other side of the highway. She panted as she skidded down the highway embankment, and a sheen of sweat froze on her skin. The stars in the black sky showed no light, and the streetlamps in town pooled light beneath them but did not illuminate far beyond their immediate radius. The darkness made the air seem colder. Lynn hoped that it would be a quiet night as she pushed open the door to the staff entrance.

"You're here!" The attending physician, Rose, was a young woman who had grown up in Nome. She handed Lynn an open case file as she entered the emergency room. Lynn took the folder, her fingers still slightly blue from the cold outside, and marveled at Rose's impervious cheer.

"Haven't heard anything from the EMTs or medevac planes," the doctor continued. "I'm going to go check inpatient, but I'll be right back. If you could look at this and present to me when I get back, that would be great. Should be pretty quiet otherwise." Rose grabbed her clipboard and disappeared into the elevator bank. Lynn took the doctor's chair and checked her phone, then opened the first patient file.

Suddenly a man in the hallway yelled "Hiya!" and the emergency room doors swung open. Lynn jumped up and rushed to the doors as they closed again, hoping to catch them before they hit whoever was on the other side. She grabbed them just in time. A bone-thin man stood just outside, bracing himself for the impact with his left shoulder while supporting a heavier, semi-conscious man with his right. Although his face was tensed in pain, Lynn recognized the second man immediately as the neighbor who had looked up at her from his kitchen window that afternoon. Dread settled in Lynn's stomach: this was the first time she had ever recognized a patient in the emergency room.

The front desk paged Rose as Lynn transferred the patient's weight onto her own shoulder, practically lifting him off the ground to guide him to a curtained private room. His companion loped after them.

"What happened?" Lynn asked as she arranged the injured man on the cot.

Her patient's friend ran his hands through his long hair and sighed up at the ceiling. "We were out on the ice, fixin' our equipment, and Brandon here opened up a steam valve aimed straight at him. Blew him against the tent and collapsed the canvas. Almost melted the ice we were standin' on. He's burned up pretty bad here — pretty bad steam burn."

"And you — you drove him here?"

"Yeah, yeah." The man nodded. "I had my truck parked out on the ice today."

By the time Rose arrived, Brandon had fainted entirely from pain. "What've we got?" she asked.

"Steam burn," Lynn said.

"Sir, could you step out?" Rose asked, gesturing toward an opening in the curtain. The man left, looking disoriented. Lynn pulled the curtain shut to block out his pacing.

Together, Lynn and Rose pulled off their patient's Carhartt jacket, work pants, long underwear, and melted wool sweater. His undershirt and boxers were stuck to his torso, so they had to cut the fabric away to reveal the burn: a swath of brutally red, puckered, blistered skin. Lynn estimated that he had second-degree burns over ten percent of his body and first-degree burns over another ten percent. While Rose checked for infection, Lynn ran for a tetanus shot, a blanket, fluids, and antibiotics. When Rose determined that they had passed the critical window, Lynn swaddled the patient in the blanket to prevent hypothermia, taking care not to disturb the IV. Rose went to fill out Brandon's Indian Health Service file, and Lynn motioned to his friend to come in through the curtain.

"Are you guys gold miners?" she asked.

"Yeah. Yeah. I know, you don't see a lot of Native miners," his friend said, slinking into the room. "I mean, I'm not Native, he is. He's from here in Nome. I'm from New Mexico."

"Um, does he have any family? He's pretty stable now, but he might have to be airlifted to Anchorage tomorrow."

"I don't know their number, but I know where his pops lives."

"Can you tell them out front? At the desk?" Lynn asked. The man nodded. "Thanks," she said.

The gold miner tipped an invisible hat and closed the curtain again.

Lynn turned back to Brandon. Brandon. His eyes were moving, pushing against the thin skin of his eyelids. His face tensed and relaxed, as if he was having a nightmare, but he was breathing without obstruction, and the IV was secure. Lynn picked her neighbor's ruined clothes off the ground, taking the time to fold Brandon's work shirt and pants before she went to find Rose. The emergency ward was quiet again. She only had a few more hours left in her shift.

Just as she turned to leave, Brandon's eyes blinked open. He stared uncomprehendingly at the fluorescent light overhead, then turned to Lynn. "Hey," he said faintly. Lynn moved to the side of his bed. Brandon gave her a small smile. "I know you. My guardian angel."

"Hi. How are you feeling?" Lynn bent to check his pupils.

"I guess I'm okay. Can you stay with me?"

"Of course," Lynn said.

"Thank you." Brandon leaned back on the pillow and closed his eyes.

Lynn watched his face carefully for a moment to see if he would wake. When his mouth loosened in sleep, she leaned over carefully to feel his forehead for a temperature. Guardian angel, she thought. Of course I can stay. A pocket of air caught in her chest next to her heart and ballooned upward into her throat and, suddenly, Lynn giggled. She felt herself smile, her first real smile in two months, and turned her eyes to the ceiling, trying to quiet the tremors in her shoulders. She giggled again, louder this time, as bubbles of elation fizzed through the dark hollow place beneath her ribs. After a few convulsive moments, she took a deep breath. A new, quieter smile started at her eyes and tugged up the corners of her lips. Holding her hand to Brandon's hot, dry face, Lynn had a vision: not of home, but of hope.

❖ ❖ ❖

annie and the talking foxes

JANE FELT HER CHIN HIT HER CHEST AND jerked her head up before her mom could yank at her arm again. "Wake up," her mom hissed. "Shit." Jane looked blearily up at her mother's pursed face, angry in the harsh porch light. Jane wanted her mom to let go of her hand — she was squeezing it so hard that Jane's fingers squished together in her mitten — but she was afraid that if her mom let go, she would leave her there, on the doorstep of an unknown house. An unknown house in Nome, the biggest city she'd ever been to, in the middle of the night.

Jane's mom hit the buzzer again, and the door opened. A lady who looked like Jane's grandma stood in front of them. Jane's eyes flew open in recognition. "Auntie Molly!" Jane yelled. "Auntie Molly, Auntie Molly,

Auntie Molly!" Her auntie gave Jane a stern look, and Jane immediately quieted.

"Come on in," Auntie Molly said wearily. Jane's mom stepped into the house and wrenched Jane's arm after her. Jane stumbled inside, and her mom reached over her and slammed the door shut. Auntie Molly locked both the locks and waited with them in the arctic entryway while Jane and her mom took off their parkas. "Sure is busy tonight," she said. "Another lady just got here too. Got in a few minutes ago." Auntie Molly raised her eyebrows at Jane's mom's boots, and Jane's mom quickly slid them off. Jane bent to undo the Velcro on her pink snow boots as fast as she could. She took off her snow pants, too, even though she was still cold from the flight. "State Trooper called ahead of time. You take her to the hospital yet?" Auntie Molly asked.

"No," Jane's mom said.

"Better do it fast, no matter what you decide to do," Auntie Molly told her. Jane's mom sighed.

"Auntie Molly, can I have a Coke please?" Jane asked. She couldn't remember the last time she'd been up so late. Auntie Molly didn't answer, but led Jane and her mom out of the arctic entry and down a hallway lined with closed doors. Jane already felt lost in the maze of the house; it looked like her school back in St. Michael. How many people lived here?

Auntie Molly opened one of the doors and turned on the fluorescent overhead light. "Here's the kitchen," Auntie Molly said. "Cupboards here and here are community, so you can take anything from them, and the ones over here are private, so if you put stuff in there you have to label it with your name. We got water and Kool-Aid for Jane."

"Kool-Aid!" Jane was so thirsty she felt like she was going to fall over at any second.

"Shh!" her mother hissed, and Jane collapsed on the ground. "Get up," her mother said. Jane sat. She wouldn't move another inch until she had some Kool-Aid. She'd come all the way from St. Michael tonight: her mom had dragged her to the airport and onto a plane, and the bush pilot had told her they had flown over one hundred miles when they landed in front of the Nome airport, and then they'd taken a taxi here. So she'd stay right on this kitchen floor if she didn't get something to drink right now.

Jane's mother kicked her on the thigh with her instep. It didn't hurt too bad, but Jane yelped anyway. "Hey!" Auntie Molly shouted. "We don't do that here! You'll have to leave."

"Won't do it again," Jane's mother mumbled, and Jane stood up.

"Can I have some Kool-Aid please?" she asked Auntie Molly.

"Your mom can get it for you. You have to drink it in the kitchen. No food's allowed outside the kitchen here."

"Okay," Jane agreed as she accepted the glass of bright red Kool-Aid her mother handed down to her.

Jane's mom sank heavily into a chair by the kitchen table and pulled out her phone. "Is there Internet here?" she asked Auntie Molly.

"We've got a computer," Auntie Molly said. Jane's mom sighed and laid her phone down on the table. Auntie Molly left the kitchen.

Jane peered out into the hallway after Auntie Molly. The door across the hallway from the kitchen was closed, but the next door was slightly open, and she could see a couple of couches. Two plastic bins full of board games and toys were stacked in the corner by the door. Jane put her Kool-Aid on the floor to take off her sweatshirt. "Pick that up!" her mom clipped at her from the table.

"Mom," Jane said, picking up the cup and walking to the table, "can we stay here? I like it here."

"Oh, baby." Jane's mom put her face in her hands and rubbed her eyes with her palms. "We can't stay here forever, but we'll stay here as long as we have to."

"Can Brother come?"

"No, Brother can't come," her mother said, pressing her eyes to the heel of her hand.

"Do I have to go to school here?"

"Maybe we'll be back in St. Michael before school starts again, or maybe you could go to school here. I have to talk to Auntie Molly."

"Mom, I don't want to go to school here."

"Well, you can't live here and go to school in St. Michael. What'ya gonna do, get on a plane every day?"

Jane giggled and saw her mom smile under her palms. "Can I fly with Uncle Jessie?"

"Uncle Jessie don't fly to Nome, honey."

"Mom, can I have some more Kool-Aid?"

Jane's mom took her palms away from her eyes. "You're already all wound up."

"Pleeeease?" Jane let her voice trail upward into a high scream. "Please please please please please?"

"Shut up," her mom said quietly. "Get the Kool-Aid yourself."

Jane hopped off her kitchen chair and skipped back to the fridge to refill her cup. Auntie Molly was back in the kitchen. "Can take you in now," she said to Jane's mother. "You got some paperwork." She glanced at Jane. "You want her to come?"

Jane's mother shook her head.

"Okay, but in the shelter the clients have to watch their kids all the time. Twenty-four seven, okay? Can't let them out of your sight unless they're at school or one of our advocates is doing an activity with them. Okay?"

"Okay." Jane's mother put her hands flat on the table and heaved herself upward. Jane saw that she had a hole near the bottom of her gray t-shirt but didn't say anything.

"You be good now," Auntie Molly said to Jane. Auntie Molly frowned at her, and Jane wondered what had happened to her kindly auntie who had baked a cake for her birthday every year when she lived in St. Michael. She didn't used to be so mean.

"Be good," Jane repeated. She put her cup of Kool-Aid carefully on the table and climbed into a chair. Her mom grabbed her phone from the table and frowned at Jane too, before following Auntie Molly out.

Jane left her Kool-Aid on the table and raced down the hallway to the room with the couches. It looked like her living room at home. She wished her friends from St. Michael were with her. They could play some of the games together. Jane saw *Sorry!*, her favorite game, but she didn't want to play by herself. She sighed, imitating her mother, and sat on one of the couches. She shoved her hands under her legs. Her jeans were too short now, and she felt a breeze between where her pants fell above her ankles and where her socks started. She wished she could wear her boots in here like she could at home, even though this house was warmer. She stood up on the couch, so she could see all the toys in the bins from overhead. Were there other kids she could play with here? She caught sight of some dolls. If there were no other kids around, she would have them all to herself. She tried not to look down the long hallway. She squished her toes against the soft couch through her socks and hummed happily.

A faint knock made Jane jump. She turned in the direction of the noise and fell backwards into the couch cushions. They were so soft that she bounced on her back a few times before sitting up. She was immediately delighted: someone to play with!

The girl in front of Jane was younger than her youngest cousin, so little she could barely stand up by herself. Unlike her youngest cousin, though, this girl didn't laugh or holler when she saw Jane. She didn't even seem to see her; instead of wanting to play, the little girl stared blankly at the top of the wall with eyes that turned black in the fluorescent light. She was wearing a white onesie with pink hearts, and her tightly-curled hair was so short that she looked like one of the plastic baby dolls Jane had at home. White gauze wrapped all the way around her forehead, hiding one of her ears. Her right hand clutched at a dirty white blanket.

"Hey!" Jane said gamely. "Hey! I'm Jane." The girl started in the direction of her voice but focused her eyes on the wall right above Jane's head. "Hey! I'm down here!" Why wouldn't she look at her? "What's your name?" The girl held the blanket up to her cheek but continued to stare over Jane's head. "What's your name?" she asked again. "Dolly? Your mom box your ears, Dolly?"

The girl's hand fell limply back to her side. She let out a low humming sound and blinked once. Jane scurried down from the couch and kneeled so close to the girl that she could almost touch the girl's cheek with her nose. The girl didn't move. "Hey!" she said, so loudly that the little girl jumped backward and almost fell on her heavy diaper. The little girl grinned widely and shook her blanket in Jane's face. All her little baby teeth were capped with metal. "Hi!" Jane squealed, but the girl's smile faded, and she looked around at the tops of the walls in confusion. "Hey!" Jane scrambled around her. "Want to play?" The girl scrunched up her face and put her blanket up to her eyes. "Don't cry!" Jane pleaded, but the girl didn't cry. She put her blanket down and resumed staring at the tops of the walls. Then she swayed her head from side to side and stared down at the floor.

Jane sat up on her knees. "Hey, wanna play Ring-Around-the-Rosie?" She held out her hand, and when the little girl didn't take it, she gently grabbed the girl's dangling wrist. The girl let Jane raise her limp arm to her face but otherwise stood still, rocking slightly on her heels. Jane didn't grab the girl's other hand — she knew from playing with her cousin that kids so young were bad at walking sideways — and started to spin. The little girl toddled around in a circle after her, trailing the white blanket on the floor. "Hey, good job!" Jane said. The other girl didn't say anything. Jane stopped spinning and opened her mouth like she was going to bite the little girl's hand, but the girl just looked at Jane's tummy and nodded her curly head.

"Jane!" her mom said sharply. Auntie Molly followed her mom into the room, still frowning. "You have to stay put."

Jane jumped and dropped the girl's arm. "Sorry! I think she's sick."

"That's Annie," Auntie Molly said. Her expression softened. "She just came in today. She's had a hard day. We'd better get her back to bed." Auntie Molly bent down and straightened Annie's onesie and wiped some drool from the side of the little girl's mouth. "Come on, let's get you back to Mom." She took Annie's unresponsive hand and gently guided her forward. The little girl rolled her head dreamily but didn't trip or let go of the blanket as Auntie Molly led her down the hallway.

"Mom, what's wrong with her?" Jane asked.

"She's probably just slow," Jane's mom said.

"Mom, can we sleep on the couch?" Jane climbed on top of the sofa and flopped down on her stomach.

"No."

Auntie Molly returned to the living room carrying a pile of sheets. "These are for you. I'll show you to your room. You guys will be in bunk beds. Maybe if some people leave you can get your own room, but there are just two of you, and we have to save the private rooms for larger families."

Jane's mom took the sheets from Auntie Molly. Auntie Molly held her hand out to Jane, who eagerly scooted off the couch to grab it. "I'll clean up the Kool-Aid tonight," Auntie Molly said, arching her eyebrow, "but you have to clean up your mess in the kitchen from now on." Jane's mom sighed.

They entered one of the rooms off the main hallway. It was completely dark, except for a window near the ceiling that let in a little light from the street lamps. Jane could barely see as Auntie Molly pointed to a set of bunk beds. She squeezed Jane's hand and whispered good night.

Jane's mom made the beds quietly and lay down on the bottom bunk, leaving Jane to climb to the top alone. Jane lay on her stomach in the dark. She could see out the window, and moved the curtain slightly to get a better view. Outside, the yellow light from the street lamps glinted against the thick snow. No one walked past the house, and in the next yard she could see two snow-go's parked outside, just like in St. Michael. Inside, it was so warm that Jane didn't even have to use her blankets. She grabbed the loose sheets with her toes contentedly and prepared to go to sleep.

Just as she closed her eyes, a soft thud against one of the bedposts at the bottom of the bunk jerked her awake. She peered over the edge of the bed and made out a small figure in the darkness, standing silently next to her sleeping mother's feet. "Annie!" Jane whispered. Annie didn't look up. Jane realized the little girl's eyes were closed. She must have sleep-walked from her bed and bumped into the bedpost. She didn't even have her blanket.

Jane scrambled down the ladder at the end of the bed. "Annie!" she whispered again. She put her hand on the little girl's shoulder to shake her awake. Annie opened her eyes slowly and stared at the top bunk above Jane's head. "Where's your mom?" Jane whispered. Annie remained completely silent. Jane looked at her own mother, who was snoring lightly in the darkness. Jane didn't want to wake her up. "Where's your bed?" she asked the little girl. No response.

Jane looked around the quiet room for an empty bed for Annie. All the bunk beds were full. "Come on. You can sleep with me." Jane lifted Annie up under the arms and held her out toward the bunk bed ladder. Instead of reaching for the ladder, Annie hung limply by her armpits. Jane realized that she would never be able to lift the little girl up to the top bunk. "Let's sleep on the couches," she said. She put Annie down, and Annie closed her eyes again. "Come on."

Jane took Annie's hand and led her out of the bedroom and through the long hallway. One of the hallway doors was open, and Jane could see the outline of a couch beneath a window. She led Annie over to the couch and hoisted the little girl up onto the cushions. Annie's eyes were open. "Time to go to sleep, Annie," Jane whispered, but Annie continued to sit straight up, staring into the darkness of the room. Jane pushed the other girl's shoulders gently downward, and she finally fell meekly toward the cushions. Annie closed her eyes. Jane patted her head.

Jane climbed onto the couch as quietly as she could and sat up on her knees to open the window curtain. She could see in the streetlight that the snow on the road didn't have any footprints or snow machine rivets, and the houses across the street were dark. Jane bounced on the couch cushions with her knees but not enough to wake Annie up. She just didn't feel like sleeping anymore.

Suddenly two red streaks broke across the shimmering road. Jane pressed her nose to the window to get a better look. The red streaks paused and materialized into foxes, knee-deep in the soft snow. "Oh!" Jane whispered. The foxes raised their noses and pranced toward the house, lifting their paws high with each step until they were standing directly under the window.

Jane felt a small hand on her shoulder and smelled the musty scent of drool. She turned and came nose-to-cheek with Annie, who leaned into her so she could stand in the sinking cushions. Her eyes, instead of roaming toward the ceiling, were focused intently on the foxes. The two animals regarded the children in the window for a moment, and then each let out a shrill, harmonious yip. Annie jumped on the couch excitedly with both feet, diaper-heavy, and yipped back.

One of the foxes nuzzled the other, and Annie clapped her hands and shrieked happily. In response, the pair of foxes separated and sat at attention before the two children. If the window were open, Jane would have been able to reach out and pet their heads. Annie pressed her forehead to the glass to look down at the animals. The larger fox let out a low growl, and Annie hummed back. Both foxes gave their tails two abrupt switches and stuck their tongues out, prompting a gurgle of delight back from Annie. Jane gazed out at the coppery animals; she had never been this close to a fox before. She put her cheek against Annie's the way her mom used to rest her cheek on Jane's when she was a baby.

"Hey!" Auntie Molly snapped the lights on, making Jane and Annie jump. "What're you two doing out here? Get back to your moms. You have to sleep."

Jane turned back toward the window. The foxes were gone. She looked at Annie, who was staring dazedly toward the ceiling. "Auntie Molly," Jane said, "Annie was talking to the foxes!"

Auntie Molly paused and raised her eyebrows. "Hmm," she said. "Well." The three stood for a moment, looking in different directions. Finally Auntie Molly said, "Time for you two to go to bed anyway." She took Annie

by the hand and helped her off the couch. The little girl followed limply, bobbing her head. Jane checked outside one last time, and, seeing nothing but empty snow, scrambled after them.

■ ■ ■

camp theresa

"IT'S NOT YOUR FAULT." MYRA TOOK HER right hand off the steering wheel and placed it firmly on Shannon's knee.

"I know it's not my fault," Shannon snapped. She stared out the passenger window at the enormous black birds that lined the telephone wires as the pickup truck passed through Front Street and emerged on to the road toward Council. "Stop saying that."

"Honey, I know you know it's not your fault, but I need you to feel that it's not your fault. Your mom was really sick. She knew it was time to go. Nothing you said could make any difference in her decision. She loved you." Myra took her hand off Shannon's knee to navigate a slippery patch of mud pooled on the unpaved highway. When the road was dry again, she glanced at Shannon and was alarmed to see tears soaking her wife's cheeks.

Shannon took a deep breath to keep from sobbing. "She was a Catholic her whole life," she mustered. "She wouldn't have done it if something hadn't made her do it."

"Shannon, honey," Myra said, pulling over to the narrow shoulder of the empty highway. "Look at me." She put her hand under Shannon's chin. "You were not that thing, okay? She loved you. She was in a lot of pain, okay? Pain made her do it, not you. You were the thing she loved most, and she kept on longer than she would have otherwise because of you. Okay?" Shannon jerked her head downward, but Myra caught her chin and held it steady. "Okay?"

"Okay," Shannon conceded. She scowled levelly at Myra for a moment, then scrunched her eyes downward toward her nose and let out a deep moan that collapsed her chest, forcing the air out of her lungs. Myra ran a hand through her short hair, then leaned over and wrapped her arms around Shannon, stretching awkwardly to avoid the steering wheel. Myra, in her role of District Attorney, had spent years practicing techniques to help herself disengage and reason through traumatic situations; now, she found that she didn't know how to participate in the emotional range that Shannon was displaying in the wake of her mother's death. She patted the back of Shannon's curly head, and Shannon buried her face in Myra's shoulder. "I just can't believe that our last conversation was about Kool-Aid," she sobbed.

"Psh, just don't worry about that," Myra said lightly. "People told her to lay off the Kool-Aid for years. And the smoking. And the twelve cups of coffee or whatever she drank every day. It was like the most normal conversation." Shannon was breathing unevenly. "We don't have to do this today," Myra said more gently. "We can come back tomorrow. Whenever you want."

"No, we have to do it today." Shannon sat up and wiped her eyes. "It's supposed to snow tomorrow, and I don't know if we're gonna have to make multiple trips or what. I don't even really know what she has out there." Shannon took a gulping breath, and Myra reached over to rub her back.

When Shannon had wiped her eyes and was breathing normally again, Myra started the truck engine and pulled off the shoulder. "Have I ever been to your mom's camp?" she asked to distract Shannon. She knew that Shannon had never invited her there; each time they drove past Theresa's small cabin on their way to their own camp, Shannon glanced at it longingly, and Myra studiously ignored the glance. "I don't remember."

"No, I never took you. I haven't even been since right after Daddy died."

"Pretty amazing that she kept it up all these years, right? Theresa was a tough cookie."

"A tough cookie who liked cookies." Shannon paused, then giggled irreverently.

Myra looked at Shannon in disbelief, then smiled. She loved the way Shannon's cheeks dimpled when she laughed. "What a bad joke!" Myra teased. "I cannot believe you're laughing at your own terrible joke."

"Shut up!" Shannon punched the dashboard radio, and the cheery voice of a KNOM DJ fumbled into the truck, which prolonged Shannon's smile for only a second longer. Myra watched her out of the corner of her eye. Shannon leaned her forehead against the truck window despite the uneven road. Here was where Theresa had picked berries, roasted hot dogs over a driftwood campfire on the beach, and reached her bare hands into the ocean to feel the hooligans, delighting in the little silver fishes that congregated by the shoreline in the summer. And here was where Shannon, just up to Theresa's knees, used to toddle after her *aaka*, her mother. Theresa had been gone for two weeks, and Myra hoped Shannon's memories of her mother on the land could overcome those of the frail woman in hospice care who could no longer feel her feet.

Shannon sighed. "Sandwich?" Myra asked. Shannon nodded, and Myra reached behind her seat to grab the cooler. "I love the Smiths, Shan, and the first fifty turkey sandwiches have been tasty, but I hope we run out of them soon, so we can go eat some real food." She passed the cooler to Shannon.

"It was nice of them to bring something," Shannon said.

"Yeah," Myra agreed quietly. "Just saying."

"I wish there had been more people there."

"There were the usual amount of people there," Myra

said. Myra and Shannon had hosted Theresa's Celebration of Life at the Nome Recreation Center the previous weekend. Shannon had invited everyone she knew, and some friends and distant family had traveled from as far away as Anchorage out of respect for Shannon and Theresa. Still, Myra did admit that attendance had been a little sparse. Every third seat or so in the gym had been empty, and half of the Nome Eskimo Dancers were in Teller for the annual dance festival there, so even the stage had seemed deserted. The well-wishers had all scattered back across Nome and Anchorage as soon as the funeral was over, without taking much time to visit, and had taken with them the bulk of Theresa's possessions. Except for the enormous tin of sandwiches, which no one had been inclined to carry with them, Myra had made sure that all the food had been redistributed as well. There wasn't any sign in their house that Theresa had even passed.

Now, however, they had to take care of Theresa's camp. The camp, a one-bedroom cabin halfway to Solomon where Theresa had spent every summer berry picking, storing fish, and sewing in private for years after her husband's death, had stood empty in her final days. When Theresa fell ill enough to be taken in at the Quyanna Care Center, the hospice in the new hospital, Shannon and Myra quietly decided to give the building and any berry buckets, crab pots, and dip nets they found inside to Myra's niece, Christina. Shannon couldn't think of anyone in her family who would want the camp; she had no brothers or sisters, and her relatives had their own camps out of town or lived too far away to keep the cabin up. Shannon just wanted to get rid of the building. Cleaning out Theresa's camp was the last logistical task that Shannon faced after her mother's death. She felt that once the camp was gone, she could focus on properly mourning her mother. Myra felt ill-prepared for that next phase, after the camp was cleaned.

"Thanks for having Courtney run the dogs for you today."

Myra pursed her lips. "Iditarod's not until March. Plenty of time to train."

"Should we call Christina?" Shannon asked. "See if she wants anything in particular?"

"My cell's already dead," Myra said.

Shannon checked her phone, then looked over her shoulder at the receding town. "Mine, too. Didn't realize we were so far out already."

The pickup truck rambled slowly over the freshly-turned dirt highway between the iron-gray sea and browning tundra. Clouds hung low over the road ahead, obscuring the eastern foothills along the cape. Snow and ice would soon make the highway impassible; most of the camps along the Nome-Council Road were already boarded up for the winter. A raindrop hit the windshield with such force that Myra jumped and clutched at the steering wheel. "Hey, what do you think of the Sitnasuak proposal?" she asked to distract herself. "I'm going to argue the other side."

"I hate this game," Shannon said. "You don't even agree with what you're saying. And what proposal? That meeting was so long."

"The one where they proposed to only rent out land for camps to Native people. And, you know, not let non-Natives pick berries or hunt or anything."

"I don't know." Shannon frowned. "I don't think that's very nice to people who come up here to work, like teachers and doctors and people who want to live here. Not welcoming-like."

"Okay," Myra said quickly, "but we have to preserve our land for us, right? What if we tried to go picking around camp, and there weren't any berries left? The spots around town are pretty bare."

"Huh. What about white folks who have Native kids? My daddy worked right with my mom when we went out to camp or hunt, and I learned a lot from him."

"Well, we'd have to make a concession."

"Lots of concessions. Can white teachers teach their students how to pick berries or find greens or whatever? Do white kids get to take those classes? You always say there needs to be more Inupiaq and Yup'ik culture in the schools."

"Yeah, taught by Native people."

"Well what about until then?"

"We've already got some local teachers, and they're great. And it's also great that non-Native folks are interested in learning about our culture. It's just an issue of resources."

"Mm." Shannon leaned her head against the window again, tired of the game.

Myra couldn't stop herself. "But remember that white

guy at the meeting who didn't even know what camp was? He was all like, 'camping, in tents?'"

"Mm-mm," Shannon said, staring out at the ocean.

"He wanted to make all our plots into one campsite that anyone could use. We had to tell him they were cabins out of town, and he said they were basically like vacation homes, that we should rent them out as timeshares. Should that guy be allowed to pick and hunt?"

Shannon sighed. "But that guy could be a really good doctor or teacher or something, and we're not even giving him a chance to understand. He'll leave as soon as he gets here." She identified the faded blue of her mother's cabin among the scattering of small houses that lined the shore of the Bering Sea and pointed at it, relieved. "There it is," she told Myra. "Turn off here."

Myra turned away from the tundra and maneuvered onto the small packed path leading to Theresa's camp. The pickup came to a stop at the white stairs in front of the cabin door. Shannon was impressed: the camp looked worn but sturdy, with a solid raised foundation not too corroded by the harsh winter or salty sea air. The stilts that jutted into the tundra to keep the cabin clear of snow and flooding looked strong.

Myra turned off the engine, and the two women sat in silence.

"How're you feeling?" Myra finally asked.

"Fine." Shannon stared straight ahead. "I can't believe I didn't really come back here after Daddy passed. I should have been helping my mom with this stuff."

"I think she liked to be by herself," Myra reminded her. "She was always happy to be at our camp before she got really bad, remember? She just needed this space."

"But she had our old house in Nome too. That's a lot of time by herself."

"You know this is different. She was on the land here."

Shannon lapsed into silence and continued to stare straight ahead. Myra took Shannon's hand and waited.

"Okay," Shannon said.

Myra leapt out of her side of the truck and rushed around the front to open Shannon's door for her. Shannon took her wife's outstretched hand and slid out the passenger side, stirring clouds of dust under her feet as she landed heavily on the dirt. Myra pulled her into another hug. Shannon let herself relax into Myra's arms and breathed in Myra's inexplicable baby-powder smell, which was a relief against the grainy desert wind. She pulled away first. Myra let her go and followed her up the stairs.

"So, what do you think is in here?" Myra asked as Shannon patted her pockets for the key.

"It's probably stinky. The last time any fish left this place was ten years ago."

"Eew." Myra plugged her nose. Shannon didn't laugh. Another drop of rain landed in her hair.

Shannon opened the cabin door.

The two women sniffed cautiously at the inside of the camp. Instead of fish, Myra detected the faint, herbal scent of incense mingled with the wood and cold sea breeze. Shannon took a deep breath. "Maybe she prayed here," she said. Myra put her hand on the small of Shannon's back, and Shannon shook her head and stepped determinedly into the cabin.

The small, square front room of the camp was neat but slightly dirty, with white plaster walls and a light blue linoleum floor. A window on each wall let in natural light, but today the gray sky made the cabin dim. Two photos were tacked unceremoniously into the plaster just below Myra's eye level near the door: a close-up of Shannon's father dip netting in the spring and a cartoony poster of Jesus Christ looking forlornly at a white light in the distance. Two white plastic chairs leaned against the back wall, adjacent to the bunk beds Shannon had slept in as a child. Battery-powered lanterns sat on the top bunk to use when night fell, if Theresa decided to come to camp at the edges of the summer months. The kitchen area had a tiny counter, a cooler, and a wood-burning stove, but no refrigerator or sink. Myra wondered how Shannon's mother had hauled water by herself all those years and thought, should I have insisted on helping out with the camp while Theresa was alive? Had Shannon expected that of me? The wind drafted through the cabin from the south window. Both women kept their jackets on.

Myra caught sight of a ripped Kool-Aid packet on one of the folding chairs and quietly picked it up before Shannon could see it. She stuffed it in her pocket. "I'll get the cleaning stuff," she offered, and backed away down the stairs to the truck. She shoved the Kool-Aid packet into the glove compartment.

"Myra!" Ethan and his little girl, Brenda, grinned at her from the flatbed of Ethan's truck. Myra frowned and shook her head, with a gesture toward Theresa's cabin.

"Just getting Theresa's stuff cleaned out," she said.

Ethan nodded. "Let me know if I can help," he said. "Weather's coming." He jutted his chin toward a fast-moving storm cloud over the cape. Myra nodded. Ethan picked up Brenda, put her on his shoulders, and disappeared into his own camp next door.

Shannon met Myra at the door when she returned to the cabin with the mop and a bucket full of cleaning supplies. "Did you see Ethan?" she asked. "Sorry I couldn't come out. I couldn't."

Myra nodded and smoothed down Shannon's curly hair. "You think she kept a lot of stuff in that shed out back?" she asked, setting the supplies down on the floor. "There's rain coming for us. We might have to get out there tomorrow." Three raindrops thudded unevenly against the south window.

"I think she had some blinds and crab baskets. I don't think she's used them since Daddy died, but I don't remember taking them out or seeing them with the other stuff at the house."

"Okay, we can try to get it all tonight." Myra leaned in to examine the photograph of Shannon's father on the wall. "Your daddy sure looks young here."

"Mom made an Inupiat out of him real quick." Shannon smiled. "That was probably the first summer they were together, right before me. She had him fishing and egging and everything."

"Where'd you get those curls?" Myra glanced at Shannon, then back at the photo. "I always thought they must've come from your daddy."

Shannon shrugged. "You know that I wouldn't have even gone to Berkeley with you, if Daddy'd had his way? He didn't think girls needed to go to college. That anyone needed to go to college. Mom made him let me go."

"Can't believe she only had you. He's handsome."

"Yeah, well. I kind of wonder if that's why she didn't have many friends, because of him. Like maybe if she'd married someone from around here or someone she met in school, she wouldn't have been so lonely."

"Can't help who we fall in love with, right?" Myra grinned broadly at Shannon, who returned a small but real smile.

"We should take a trip down to California," Shannon said. "His family sure loved my mom."

"I like this plan. Let's get camp cleaned up, and we'll take a vacation after Iditarod." Myra unloaded the bucket and started mixing apple cider vinegar into the water. The spattering of raindrops against the window evolved into a steady downpour as Shannon pulled on gloves to scrub the inside of the cooler.

"You haven't been back to Teller for a while," Myra said, after a few minutes of silence. "It's so close. We should go visit."

"Only you have family in Teller," Shannon reminded her. "My mom was only at Holy Trinity for boarding school. Nobody from my side moved to Teller to be near her when she was there, and she came straight to Nome after."

"I wish I'd asked my mom more about being at boarding school at Wrangell," Myra said. "What it was really like when she was there. She didn't talk about it so much."

"Mom used to tell me things," Shannon said. "But it's like her life didn't start until she was eighteen and back in Nome."

"Well that's when she met your dad and had you, right? That summer of love probably had something to do with it."

Shannon raised her eyebrows at Myra's teasing. "I should have had her stories recorded or something," she said. "I bet KNOM would have let me use their studios. Mom used to love telling about how one of the priests always brought them apples for dessert. She had a bunch of stories like that."

"Psh, who needs apples when they could have been eating *muktuk*? That boarding school food must have been nasty. What'd white people eat in the fifties? Jello?" Myra watched Shannon's face tighten and knew she had made a mistake: she'd gotten Shannon thinking about Kool-Aid again. "Our food is better for you anyways," Myra said, trying to recover.

Shannon sniffed. "I don't know. She never told me."

"At least she met your godmother there. Wasn't Molly from St. Michael? They might not have ever met without school."

"Yeah."

"Is she still liking Nome? That was a pretty big move for her."

"We have to go visit." Shannon sighed and brushed the dust off the front of her jeans. "Guess my mom wouldn't have even had this camp without her. She used to tell Mom stories about growing up with camp when they were in school, and Mom got really into it, making sure she built a cabin when she moved back here. I guess my mom's family didn't have camp. She said they just stayed in Nome." Shannon sat back on her heels. "Man, I could have grown up without camp."

"My mom couldn't go back to Shishmaref after she graduated Wrangell. Shish felt too weird for her, I guess. She wasn't used to living with her family anymore and didn't like the food there or anything. She had to move to Anchorage."

"Well, if she'd stayed in Shish she wouldn't have met your daddy, and I wouldn't have met you!" Shannon grinned at Myra. Myra smiled back, glad that the cleaning seemed to be doing some good.

The women scrubbed in silence, sweating in the cold air. The cabin brightened as Shannon and Myra wiped off thin coats of black dust from the floor and walls. Myra shook out two large black trash bags to collect the cleaning rags and papers that had steadily collected mold since Theresa went into hospice care, and as night fell, the cabin began to look empty.

Shannon turned on the electric lanterns on the top bunk bed. "We could probably make it to our camp tonight, if we left now," she said. "We could stay there overnight."

"I have to go back and make sure Courtney fed the dogs," Myra reminded her. She stood and stretched, grazing her fingertips against the cabin ceiling. "Let's just finish the inside here and go back to town."

"Okay," Shannon said. "I can check the rest of the stuff and fix it up for winter tomorrow."

"I'll go with you. Sorry those dogs are such divas. Maybe it won't snow now that it's raining like this, and tomorrow won't be too bad. It's still so warm."

"Too warm."

"Might tear up the road though."

"That's why we got four-wheel."

The rain grew louder.

"You want to do your mom's room now?" Myra asked gently.

Shannon sank onto the bottom bunk. "In a minute," she said. "I've actually never been in there. I know, right? Camp's so small now."

"It was her place." Myra sat down next to her, and the mattress springs creaked in protest. "These beds sure have been here since you were a kid," she sighed. She put her arm around Shannon's shoulders. Raindrops pounded steadily against each of the four windows, black in the lamplight.

Finally, Shannon put her hands on her knees and pushed herself off the bed. "Give me a couple minutes," she said. Myra nodded and stood, taking one of the lanterns.

There was no knob on Theresa's bedroom door, and the hole where the lock should have been was taped over on the inside to block out the sunlight on summer nights. Shannon put her finger in the ridge of the lock hole and eased the door open. A rush of stale incense and her mother's smell, a warm blend of fabric softener and sand, swept past Shannon and into the rest of the cabin.

"Whew!" Myra said. "I feel like I'm in church!"

Myra handed the lantern to Shannon, who held the light high and cast stark shadows in the short, narrow space. The lantern revealed a single bed, encased in off-white sheets and a dark blue comforter. A low wooden table stood next to the bed, capped with a faded Dean Koontz novel and a cup of cold coffee. A stack of magazines and *Nome Nuggets* piled against the left wall, and a pair of sweatpants and a Nome Nanooks high school t-shirt lay crumpled on the floor. It looked as if Theresa had expected to return to the cabin. Both women raised their eyebrows in surprise at the beautiful seal skin stretched out on a frame of driftwood that hung on the wall behind the bed.

"Is that from your dad?" Myra asked. "He'd had to have gotten it before 1972."

"I guess he could have. I've never seen it before," Shannon said. She wiped at her eyes impatiently. "Hey, I can do this. Do you want a magazine?"

Myra nodded. "I'll be right here."

Shannon handed Myra a magazine from the top of the pile, and Myra sat heavily on the lower bunk in the living room. She flipped through the pages, listening into the next room for signs of grief, but all she heard was Shannon stripping the sheets off the bed, taking the seal skin frame down from the wall, and sweeping. After a while, Myra kicked her legs to gain the momentum she needed to stand up off the sagging mattress and stretch.

A scraping sound on the floor made Myra look down. A piece of paper clung to the bottom of her rain boot, a newspaper clipping now that she bent to look at it. She picked the clipping off the sole of her boot, careful not to rip it. A tack stuck through the article, and a little bit of plaster clung to its sharp tip. The article itself was nonsensical, cut in half. Myra turned the paper over to reveal a photograph of a middle-aged white man. He grinned out at Myra through a mop of perfect curls that fell just over the top of his clergy collar. Although Myra could see the old hospital in Nome behind him, she didn't recognize the priest. The caption read, "Father Amos spends the winter teaching at Holy Trinity and enjoys fishing in Nome during the summer."

"Hey, Shannon," Myra called.

"What?" Shannon stuck her head out of her mother's bedroom. A streak of black dust covered one cheekbone, and her hair coiled around her ears.

"Never mind," Myra said. "Just this stupid fashion magazine. I'll tell you about it later."

"Okay. I'm almost done."

"Take your time," Myra said. Shannon disappeared back into Theresa's room.

Myra stared down at the picture in her hand, then stuck it between the pages of the magazine and shoved the magazine into one of the large black trash bags. If Shannon asked about the magazine later, Myra would tell her she had forgotten about it, that it hadn't been important anyway.

❖ ❖ ❖

the muskoxen

ALICE COULD TELL THAT HER DOG TEAM was nervous. Their noses, which had been kept low to the ground in concentrated pursuit of their peers on the Iditarod trail for over a week, now popped up anxiously to sniff at the cold spring air as they raced over the snowy tundra toward the finish line in Nome. Alice wearily surveyed the vast white plain that dwarfed her dark, stealthy team of eight. Not for the first time in the race, she wished that she had a seat on the back of her sled so that she could rest.

"Jester Jester Jester!" she called. Jester, her favorite wheel dog, snapped his nose out of the air, grinned back at her, then stuck his face in his teammate Jackie's butt. Jackie gave a mute start of surprise and jerked into Prince, the dog in front of him on the line.

"Jackie Jackie Jackie!" Alice crooned. Jackie was another favorite because he reminded Alice of her oldest daughter when she was a toddler: tough and independent but in constant need of gentle guidance. Her daughter was still like that, Alice mused. Jackie drew his ears back gratefully and steadied his pace. Duchess, to Jackie's immediate left, squatted as she ran and expelled a wide trail of shit. "Duchess Duchess Duchess!" Alice chanted as the sled runners passed over her dog's excrement. Alice absently noted that Duchess's feces were worm-free and a healthy shade of brown. "Good job, Duchess." She wondered if she would be able to communicate normally with other humans when she finally reached Nome; after ten days on the trail, she couldn't imagine not congratulating something every time it pooped. Dog mushing, she supposed, was like motherhood in more ways than one.

Alice let her eyelids droop. She was grateful for the soft snowy desert under her sled runners after jolting through so many days on the rocky and semi-melted terrain of the state interior. Her team, she felt, could handle a little less direction from her for this final stretch. The shadowed mountains ahead of them rose nearer out of the plain, and beyond those mountains Alice would finally be able to see Nome, where the Burled Arch on Front Street marked the end of the trail. The faint smell of over two hundred dogs kenneled less than twenty miles away accounted for her own team's skittishness, she was sure, but that smell would also guide them into town. Her sled was light, as she had eaten or shed most of her supplies at checkpoints along the race route, and the runners sailed along smoothly behind her team. Alice's dogs continued to test the dry air with their noses, occasionally straining at their harnesses on the line but not enough to throw off the rhythm of their teammates. Loose coils of snow caught the pale March sunlight and drifted ahead toward the cerulean mountains that signaled the end of the plain.

Alice sighed happily. When she had left Safety Sound, the last checkpoint on the Iditarod trail on the way to Nome, she had been in thirtieth place. Her goal at the beginning of the season had been to finish the race in the top twenty-five, but she had adjusted her expectations after her fastest lead dog, Knightly, had started to act erratically. Rather than risk her dogs' safety as they got tired, Alice had dropped off Knightly and seven more of her original team of sixteen dogs at various checkpoints along the race route. They would be cared for and flown back to Anchorage, where she would see them in just a few days.

The eight dogs remaining with her on the trail had impressed Alice with their fitness and discipline through-out the last leg of the race. Alice had grown to love these dogs over her short year and a half of training, and had invested a small fortune to ensure that they ate the high-est quality food she could afford and wore the vests and durable Cordura booties that protected them from the Alaskan winter. She would be sad to sell them to another musher, but this would be her last race, and these dogs got depressed and angry if they didn't trot through a marathon every couple of days. Children grow up; you can't keep them with you forever. And, she thought, thirtieth place was not bad for a first Iditarod. With only eighteen miles to go until she crossed the finish line, Alice was already beginning to plan how she would recount the journey to her husband and daughters in Nome: see, your old mom can learn some new tricks yet.

Alice glanced behind her. There wasn't another musher in sight. She quietly celebrated her secure thirtieth place finish with a call to her team: "Jester! Jackie! Prince! Kingly! Queenie! Reign! Duchess! Duke! Duke Duke Duke!" Each dog flopped their ears backward in appreciation and stuck their tongue out.

"Alice Alice Alice," a tiny voice repeated behind her. Alice ignored it. The phantom call was just her tired, lonely brain interpreting the skid of her runners against the snow as a familiar sound. It was the same voice that had called to her during her twenty-fifth straight hour in the operating room during her medical residency all those years ago. She had ignored it then, too, and look at her now: a successful surgical practice, an impending retirement, and, this Iditarod adventure had proven to her, plenty of years left to relax at home in Wisconsin, and enjoy all the things she'd missed while she was working. She realigned her grip on the sled handlebars and leaned back on her heels to relieve her aching hips and knees. Alice closed her eyes and imagined the warm bed, shower, and food that awaited her. Maybe her husband had found a charming gold rush era hotel where they could whisper to each other under a warm, goose-down blanket.

Suddenly, Alice realized that she was no longer moving. She opened her eyes. The team had stopped and were milling anxiously around the line, except for her lead dogs, Reign and Queenie, who stood alert, pointing ahead.

Alice kicked the sled brake into the snow and hopped off the sled. Reign and Queenie trembled at the front of the line as she approached. "Reign Reign Reign," she said gently. "What is it? What is it, Reign?" She held out her hand, but the dog drew back and bared his teeth. "Reign!" she said sternly, straightening to her full height. Be the Alpha, she thought as she stared the dog down. Jackie barked from the middle of the line. Reign held Alice's gaze for a moment, then broke eye contact and hurled himself sideways into Queenie, who yelped and stumbled to the right. The smaller dog recovered quickly and crouched low to the ground, preventing her partner from turning the team around. Alice grabbed the line and pulled both dogs forward by their harnesses. She couldn't believe that one of her most reliable team members was sabotaging the race. Reign whined back at her and rolled his eyes pitifully.

Alice knelt and vigorously rubbed Reign's neck and ears. When he finally quieted, she turned her head to rest against the scruff of the dog's neck, above his vest. She blinked slowly behind her sunglasses, feeling her energy melt out of her body and into the snow. Vaguely she thought if she stayed here like this she would freeze to death, and it would be silly to freeze to death so close to the end of the Iditarod trail. She had to get moving. She had to. Her daughters were waiting for her, and her husband.

A chorus of barks from the middle of the line woke her moments later. She opened her eyes and felt her chest clench in fear. Two hundred feet from the front of the line, directly between the trail markers, stood a herd of muskoxen. Alice had never seen muskoxen up close. They were enormous. Their winter coats gave their woolly brown shoulders and backs a silver sheen in the pale sun. She counted fourteen muscled, buffalo-sized animals standing in the snow. Their eyes were black pits behind their curled horns, horns that could run through a sled dog as if the dog were made of butter. But Alice knew the real danger came from their hammer-flat hooves, which would trample her and her entire team if any of the beasts got spooked by an overly-energetic dog. Steam rose above the herd as their gargantuan, prehistoric bodies expanded and contracted with each breath, and they groaned a deep bass sigh that ground visibly on the dogs' ears. The muskoxen were staring at Reign. Their tails were up, signaling a charge.

Alice's team began to growl. "Jester! Jackie! Prince! Kingly! Queenie! ReignDuchessDuke," Alice whispered, aware that these could be her last words. She had to keep the dogs calm. "Good dogs. Good dogs. Good dogs. Jester. Prince. Queenie. Queenie Queenie Queenie." A great shudder ran through the muskox herd as each animal shook its shaggy, matted head and shoulders. Reign whined and tried to crouch behind Queenie. Queenie pulled weakly at the line.

Alice rose carefully and kept her eyes on both sets of animals as she backed slowly down the line. She decided that she could not put her team in danger by attempting to retreat or go around the herd. Better, she thought, to stay put and wait until the muskoxen lost interest and wandered away. Alice was encouraged that the herd had not moved closer to the lead dogs, and despite their nervous shuffling, the dogs had not rushed or heckled the mammoth beasts. The standoff could not last much longer.

Still, Alice found her handgun at the top of her sled bag. She wished she had thought to practice a little more often before the race. She tested the safety, and the metallic clicks sounded like shots over the barren tundra. Her dogs whined, and the low panting of the muskoxen grew louder, but when Alice straightened she saw that both her team and the herd were stationary. Reign bit softly at Queenie over the line, but Queenie ignored him. Alice felt the weight of her gun and knew that it would only cause the muskoxen to charge.

"Trail!" a voice behind Alice called. "Trail!" Alice's heart jumped in her chest — I'm having a heart attack, she thought — and she dropped the gun onto her sled runners. It bounced harmlessly and lodged into the snow.

Another dog team pulled up beside hers.

"Alright?" Alice recognized the musher. She was another rookie, a younger local woman from Nome.

Seven dogs on a line pulled up next to Alice's team, and another dog grinned up at her from the other musher's sled pouch. Reign and Queenie instantly relaxed and wagged their tails at their competitors. The musher took off her goggles and peered concernedly at Alice through her balaclava.

"Ehm," Alice said, pulling down her own face mask. "The muskoxen." She pointed at the herd, which quivered directly in front of them.

"What?" the other musher shouted. "Gee, you're shaking. Have some of my water. It's still warm." She pulled out a thermos and Alice took it with her ungloved hand. "Almost there, now."

"Thanks," Alice said uncertainly. She took a drink and handed the thermos back. She could see the muskoxen staring at the dog teams out of the corner of her eye.

"No problem. I'm Myra, by the way." The musher pulled her goggles back on. "You good? Good. See you in Nome. Hike hike!" Her dogs leapt forward at the signal to run. Alice clung to her sled runners as Myra's dogs padded confidently toward the muskox herd, which regarded her team disinterestedly. Myra's lead dog approached the largest muskox and, without hesitation, sped straight through the animal's front legs.

Suddenly the illusion dissolved. The silver-backed herd shimmered before Alice's eyes and evaporated from the land. Alice watched the back of Myra's black parka surge toward the blue mountains. In half a blink, the herd was gone, and the only marks on the trail were the sleek lines of the sled runners that had conquered the trail before her and the tiny paw prints of the dog teams ahead. The sun brushed the top of the mountain range, sending long indigo shadows onto the plain. Alice looked behind her; another musher was approaching in the distance.

Alice shook her head, mourning the loss of her top thirty finish. Foolish old woman, she thought. She picked up her gun, put it back in the sled bag, and pulled on her glove. Her dogs looked back at her over their shoulders. She wiped her nose and smiled tearfully at her team; they would have another chance to win next year. "Jester! Jackie! Prince! Kingly! Queenie! Reign! Duchess! Duke!" she called thickly. "Hike hike!"

■ ■ ■

pool

CRACK.

The cue ball slammed into the ten, knocking it smoothly into the left corner pocket of the pool table. Matt didn't have to move to sink the eight; the cue ball sent it sailing into the right corner, and the game was over. Great game, great game, a round of beers for everyone. Both teams had shot their best and played with excellent sportsmanship. Both teams had also only consisted of one player: Matt.

Matt racked his cue and sauntered over to the empty bar. The pretty bartender was working today. She was the only person who could have seen that game, and she'd been washing dishes the whole time. Nothing to worry about. Matt wasn't going to play against any of her friends anyway.

"Hey, sweetheart," he said when she came over. "Beer and a shot."

The pretty bartender grabbed a bottle without answering, popped it open, and put it on the counter. "I got a tab," Matt said as she poured him some whiskey. He took the shot and left a little gold piece, one of his last flakes, on the bar for her. The good Lord knew he probably owed her a few tips, and he needed her to be on his side if anything happened.

Matt sipped his beer and stared at the empty pool table, then went out on the back porch for a smoke. It was a beautiful day, perfect for mining: calm wind, high visibility, steady waters. The Bering Sea was littered with small dredges, each of which supported a diver vacuuming gold off the sea floor. Matt wished he was out there with them.

From the porch, Matt could see over the rocky sea wall and directly into the cabin of Brandon's dredge. Brandon was Matt's best friend; the two had met right there in Breakers Bar when they were both eighteen years old. Matt could see Brandon climbing into his wet suit on the dredge, but he couldn't see who was tending.

Matt lit an American Legend. He'd discovered upon his arrival that Nome's roads weren't paved in gold, and that Nome was more similar to his hometown of Gallup, New Mexico, than he'd ever dreamed possible. Plus, he'd gotten there too early in the season; the ice was just breaking up on the ocean, and it was too dangerous to mine. But Brandon had let him sleep in the tiny stand-alone house his family kept on the outskirts of town that first night, since it was a weekday and nobody was using it, and he'd hooked Matt up with a construction job the very next week. When the Bering Sea thawed and they'd fixed up Brandon's vessel, Brandon had let Matt use his dredge to dive. Brandon had taught Matt all he knew about gold mining, and the two had spent every waking minute together even when Matt started to make enough to rent his own place. Matt had never had a friend like Brandon, so close they could be brothers.

Not my brother, Matt told himself. Your brother doesn't fall asleep while tending, doesn't leave you under-water when his faulty oxygen tank sputters, doesn't fail to acknowledge that he almost killed you when you finally claw your way to the surface. And then, espe-cially, he doesn't demand that you pay him for his trou-bles. If that was a brother, Matt was glad he hadn't been born with one in the first place. Never mind that they hadn't bothered to install a carbon monoxide detector in their tent.

Truth was, Matt could be as mad about Brandon's neg-ligence as he could muster, but the dredge still belonged to Brandon. He'd had a pretty sweet deal for a while — dredge owners could easily sink their whole cleanup into maintaining a vessel — but now his mining career was over. Without access to Brandon's dredge, the only way Matt could mine would be by panning the creeks, and in his humble opinion only drug addicts and dreamers thought there was still gold on the land. Matt still needed money to live on, though, so he had decided to put one of his other talents to use: playing pool.

Matt had thought out his strategy last night. He wasn't going to play against his friends or the Natives or the people who worked at Kawerak or Sitnasuak or the schools or the hospital. No, he'd play against the haphazard wanna-be gold miner adventurer types who came to Nome with their entire savings and left with nothing anyway. It was early in the season; the richest folks hadn't yet lost all their money building faulty dredges or buying permits or getting swindled on equipment sales, only to find out that gold mining was boring, tiring, and nowhere near the *Bering Sea Gold* shit or whatever they'd envisioned on their plane ride from Anchorage to Nome. They were still optimistic, they were still rich, and they still thought that they could outsmart a real gold miner from his daily wage.

It was five o'clock in the evening, and the sun was high in the sky. Matt pitched his cigarette off the porch and returned to the bar's dim, fluorescent light. The glow at the front of the bar, where the pretty bartender served drinks, was warm and inviting, while the games area in the back was harsh and stale. Matt had been hanging out at the back of the bar since his step-daddy started taking him along on his nightly binges when he was five years old, until he started to feel more comfortable with the fluorescent buzz in his ear than without. A few Natives shuffled into the front of the bar and bowed their heads toward the pretty bartender. They didn't glance at Matt when he took a seat on one of the bar stools.

Matt's buddy Ryan was the first miner in the bar. "What's good, Matty?" Ryan asked as he took a seat next to his friend and ordered a PBR. "Heard about Brandon, man. Fuckin' asshole. You could've died."

"Jesus, I know. I felt like I was chokin' down there." Matt held his hands to his throat and bugged out his eyes. "Couldn't see a goddamn thing – had to leave the vacuum down there, and now it's damaged as shit. Brandon wants me to fuckin' pay for it."

"You gotta be kidding me. Fuckin' asshole." Ryan downed half his can. "I'm probably out for the rest of the season too. My goddamn water heater broke. How the fuck am I supposed to dive? Fuckin' freezing down there."

"Take it to Andy's. He'll probably do it for free."

Ryan shook his head. "No way. You hear he fucked Jess?"

"Fuckin' cunt."

"They're both fuckin' cunts." Ryan finished his beer and ordered another. "Wanna play darts?"

Matt shrugged. He couldn't aim at a dartboard to save his life. Usually he didn't mind: he'd lose at darts and hand out American Legends, and in return, the other miners would give him fish and meat when he'd had a bad season or let him help repair their dredges for an extra buck. But right now he needed some cash. "Just gonna sit here for a minute," Matt said. "Might try out some pool tonight."

"You tryin'a find a different way to lose money? Get outta here, broke-ass. You ain't even got a dredge to fix."

"Suck my dick, Ryan." Matt let his voice rise. He was a nice guy, but he wasn't going to let his friend go too far. When Ryan looked cowed enough, Matt looked down, pretending he had something on his flannel that he had to brush off, then took another sip of beer.

A hand slammed down on Matt's shoulder. "Matty," thundered Keith, the enormous red-bearded miner. "Heard you're looking for a new dredge."

"Sure am, after Brandon almost fuckin' killed me."

"Can't trust nobody around here, Matt. Jason just tried to claim more than his fair share of the gold from our cleanup today, so I booted him. We need another hand. We're going out tomorrow morning."

"Sure, I'll try for a day. Thank you, sir."

"Nine A.M. at the port. And I mean fuckin' nine A.M. None of this afternoon shit. Gold's all gone by the afternoon."

"It don't work that way, Keith."

"Sure fuckin' does. Gotta get on the gold before some new motherfuckers come and steal it." Keith grabbed his beer and ambled toward the back of the bar. Ryan trailed after him. Matt knew Keith was bluffing — Keith hadn't been out all season. He made his money as a trader and was too embarrassed to admit that he hadn't made it mining gold. A lot of guys were ashamed.

It was almost six, and Breakers was starting to fill up. Matt adjusted the long sleeves of his flannel shirt and brushed through his hair with his fingers. He wondered if he should have shaved. People always told him he looked like a teenager 'cause he was so skinny, so he usually only shaved once a week. Tonight, though, he wanted to look a little fresh. He wished he didn't have to wash his clothes in the sink of his tiny house; even his nicest shirt smelled like sweat and saltwater. He used the back of his cuffs to dab at his forehead and shook the hair out of his eyes to get a clearer view of the bar. Matt waited so long he had begun to consider a game of darts when the man he was looking for came through the door.

"Dan, over here!" Matt gestured to the empty barstool next to him. "Lemme buy you a beer."

"Thanks, Matt." Matt eyed Danny's nice watch, clean sneakers, and tailored jeans as he slid onto the empty stool and nodded at the pretty bartender. Danny'd just graduated from college that summer and had come to Alaska to stay with his cousin, Andy, at the shop and do a little mining. There had been a little grumbling that the *Bering Sea Gold* producers would recruit him to be on the show just because of his Superman curls and cleft chin, and then someone would have to let him work on their dredge for the season. Matt could not believe he and Danny were the same age and that Danny was just cashing his first checks at the bank. While the other loose-limbed miners cavorted, sprawled, flexed, and lounged around the bar, the jukebox, and the back games section in their work-worn overalls, Danny sat upright on his barstool with a smile plastered on his Ken Doll face. If he weren't Andy's cousin, he'd have been beaten to a pulp already.

"How's Nome treatin' ya, Dan?" Matt asked jovially.

"Ah, love it, man!" Danny said. "I'm thinking of staying past the summer — might see what winter's like, get a job at Kawerak or something."

"Glad to hear it. We need smart people such as yourself around here. You findin' any gold?"

"Not yet. They say most people start out slow though, so I'm not too worried."

"Yeah, I didn't get anything when I first started diving either." That was a lie. Matt had had beginner's luck, which had hooked him on mining as soon as he'd cleaned his first gold pan. The exhilaration of getting on the gold kept him coming back, and the thrill of the few cleanups he had were worth the endless shifts on the dredge.

"Finish your beer?" Danny asked. "I'll get next round."

"Thankya." Two Alaskan Whites appeared immediately; the pretty bartender knew Danny tipped well. "I heard you got some pool skills," Matt said. "I been losin' at darts for months, and I'm broke as shit. I need a new game." He casually brushed an imaginary bit of dust off the front of his shirt. "Teach me to play?"

"Oh yeah, sure thing." Danny stood and stretched, revealing an abdomen chiseled by his college swim team and good eating. Matt knew he could have that stomach too, if he could afford more protein. "Looks like the table's free."

Matt followed Danny to the back of the bar. Ryan, Keith, and some of the other miners that had hopped over the porch to come in the back way, eyed Matt with amusement or suspicion. Matt knew he looked like a sucker, but he grunted gamely when Ryan slapped him on the back. "Learnin' you some pool, Matty?" he drawled in his exaggerated southern accent. He played extra hick when the rich guys were around.

"Suck it, Ryan."

"Suit yourself. I get first game when he's done teaching you. I need some beer money."

"Suck. It."

"Okay," Danny said as he began to set up the game. "So each player gets a set of balls, right."

"Balls!" Ryan yelled, and swung a dart into the bullseye without even looking at the board.

"I said shut up!" Matt roared. He turned to Danny, who looked unnerved, and gave him a friendly smile. "Now, you were saying, Dan?"

"Right. So one player gets the solid colors, and one player gets the striped ones. And you rack them all into a triangle, like this." Matt could practically feel the other man's ears burning, they were so red. "And then you break the triangle with the white, um, ball, and you try to get your set into the pockets. But don't hit the eight-ball into the pocket — if you pocket the eight-ball before you get all your, um, balls into the pockets first, you lose. If you pocket the eight-ball after your set is off the table, you win. Got it?"

Matt studied the table and rubbed his scruffy chin as if deep in thought. "Do I use the white ball every time I hit another ball?"

"Yeah, you have to use that one. Here's a pool cue. Hold it like this." Danny leaned over the table and Ryan humped the air behind his ass. Danny's neck was as red as Cherry Kool-Aid, but he didn't turn around. "Got it?"

"Yeah, I think I got it. I'll probably ask more once we get to playin'."

"Lemme get some more beers. Ryan?"

"Huh? Oh, yeah." Ryan hurled another dart at the board and almost impaled a Native guy going out for a cigarette. "Fuck."

Matt pretended to line up the cue ball, and Danny was back within seconds. It took most of the other miners forever to get a beer. Goddamn rich boy.

"Ready to play? You can break, since it's your first time."

"So line it up like this?"

"Yeah, but don't hold the cue like that. Hold it lower. You might have to squat down to see how it lines up with the ball." Matt's first pass glanced off the cue ball, sending it slightly to the left. "No worries, man," Danny said lightly as Ryan snickered. "Let's just start the game over. It's like gold mining — it takes a little while to get used to. Once you get the hang of it, though, you'll have it in your muscle memory."

"Muscles got memories?" Ryan asked in false earnestness.

"Yeah," Danny said slowly, like he was talking to a little kid. "They remember independently of your brain how to do things. It's how you know how to ride a bike every time you get on one."

Ryan rolled his eyes at Matt. "Yeah, well Matt here don't know how to ride no bike."

"Yes I do, ya stupid SOB. Now shut up! I'm concentratin'!" Matt stuck his tongue out and clenched his teeth around it. The cue ball missed the tip of the rack by inches.

The game that followed was the slowest game of Matt's entire life. He hadn't even played that poorly when he was a kid. Every shot he made just barely scraped the ball, and he made sure he only occasionally got one in the pocket. Danny was practically slobbering with encouragement. Matt thought that if Danny had been a decent pool player himself, the game would have ended much sooner. When Danny sunk the eight-ball, Matt turned to the miners crowded around the game and bowed. The miners laughed, slapped their knees, and snapped the suspenders of their Carhartt jumpsuits at him.

Ryan swaggered over. "Time to go back to darts, huh?"

"I'ma get another beer." Matt stormed off to the bar. He didn't have to pretend to feel frustrated and angry; that had been the first game he'd lost in years, and he could easily get worked up about that humiliation.

"Alrighty. I got next game!" Ryan shouted after him.

The front door to Breakers blew open, and two women poured into the overheated bar. It was a warm day in Nome, but these girls looked like they were dressed to go out in Miami: one was wearing heels, the other had on short shorts and a sheer top. Both had smeared makeup all over their faces, but the makeup didn't cover up the fact that they were pretty. The one in heels had long reddish hair that brushed against the top of her jeans and an upturned nose perfectly centered on her slim face; the other had short dark hair and a round face like a doll. They giggled as all heads turned toward them, then sauntered to the middle of the bar. "Matt!" the dark-haired girl called. "Get over here!"

Matt put on his biggest grin and sidled over. "Ladies," he said. "How are you both this fine evening?"

"Better now that we've seen you," the redhead, Suze, giggled. "You clean up today?"

"Nah, I took the day off." No need to go into his fight with Brandon. The other girl, Lynn, would probably hear it from Brandon's side and then tell Suze, and then Matt wouldn't have a chance with her. Matt's smile faded. "Can you ladies do me a favor?" he asked quickly. "Sit here and drink these vodka cranberries I'm about to buy you, and come over to the pool table when I'm done playing Ryan. I'm gonna play my best game yet."

"Oh, we'll be there," Suze said. She was already flushed and couldn't seem to stop laughing. "We'll come over when we finish our drinks, don't worry."

"I just don't want you to see my practice round. Gotta be on my game." The truth was Suze and Lynn scared the shit out of Matt. He'd never really been friends with any girls who wore the kinds of clothes they wore, and he couldn't think of anything he might have in common with them. Instead of talking, he tried to think of something to do with them. Well, he could think of a few things to do, but he didn't think they'd agree to them yet. Suze saw him as something of a hero: he'd rescued her from a game of darts with some rowdy seasonal miners just a few days ago. When she found out he was Brandon's friend, she'd let him put his arm around her waist. So that was good. Watching the game would be something. He wondered what it was like to sleep with someone who worked in a hospital — she'd probably learned a thing or two about anatomy there.

"Go get 'em, Matt," Suze said, punching Matt's shoulder playfully.

Matt slapped a twenty-dollar bill on the bar. "See you ladies in about fifteen minutes. Keep an eye out. Gimme a kiss for good luck." He held his cheek out to Suze, who kissed his scraggly face and giggled again. She'd probably never kissed a gold miner before.

"Oooee!" Ryan whooped as Matt ambled to the back of the bar. "Matt's gettin' lucky tonight!"

"Shut up, asshole."

"What's with you? Gettin' some pussy ain't a bad thing." The miners around the pool table growled in agreement. "Holy shit. What're we bettin'?"

"Twenty-five?"

"Twenty-five! Are you fuckin' kidding me? I ain't wastin' my time on a twenty-five dollar game of pool."

"You know you're gonna win, shithead. Come on, gimme a break. I got no cleanup."

"A hundred. You ain't gonna get better unless you got some motivation."

"I got plenty motivation." Matt jerked his head at Lynn and Suze, who were pretending to have a conversation but were sneaking covert glances at the pool table.

"Ain't enough," Ryan slurred. "I ain't playin' for less than fifty."

"Fine. Thirty-five." Matt racked the balls clumsily and tossed Ryan a quarter. "Wanna flip?"

Ryan called heads and won, and his cue ball rang straight and true. The rest of the balls scattered, and the nine sunk into the right middle pocket.

"So you've got solids, then, right?"

"That's right. Let's see you hit something."

This game was better. Matt hit almost every ball but just missed the pockets, and every time a ball didn't sink he let himself get a little wilder. "Mo-ther-fucker!" he yelled. "Sonofabitch! I almost had it!"

"It just takes a little while to get used to," Ryan said, mimicking Danny's proper grammar. "You'll get the hang of it, I'm sure. Little bitch," he added. "That thirty-five's mine." He sank the last ball. The crowd around the table clinked their bottles together and stamped their feet. A few of them swayed on their stools with the commotion and caught themselves just as they teetered too far.

"Fuck!" Matt muttered. "Fuck fuck fuck fuck fuck."

Lynn and Suze traipsed over right on cue. Suze put her hand on Matt's bicep, and he flexed a little so she could feel the muscle through his shirt. "What's wrong, Matt?"

"Lost a game of pool to this fucker over here," Matt said. He couldn't help but burst into a full-toothed grin. "I gotta redeem myself, make some money to buy you ladies drinks. Who's next?"

"You fuckin' kidding me?" Ryan asked. "You're terrible. Girls, you gotta be with somebody who can actually play the game." He put his arm around Suze. "Hey, little lady. I got a song for you. You ever seen a tundra goose?" Suze smiled tightly and widened her eyes at Lynn. Ryan was cheerfully undeterred. "Ready? It goes, 'My mama shot a tundra goose 'cause it was a-shittin' in her orange juice —'"

"Jesus Christ." Matt knew he'd had too many beers; he was actually starting to feel angry now. "I can fuckin' play. I said, who's next?"

"I'll go." Danny actually raised his hand like they were all in first grade. "How much?"

Matt slammed his fist down on the pool table. "Two hundred!"

"Are you serious? I'd feel bad."

"No, I mean it. This asshole" — Matt jerked his head toward Ryan — "is fuckin' right, I gotta get me some motivation. My motivation'll be taking this lady right here out to dinner tomorrow night."

"I don't wanna take your money, man."

"Let's just fuckin' bet two hundred. Fuck."

"Fine, man. Your money." Danny racked the balls and Matt winked at Suze. Suze smiled back, but her eyes looked concerned. Lynn was trying to catch a glimpse of Brandon's dredge out the back door. The men around the table drifted away to get more beer. Dan pulled out a quarter from his back pocket. "Call it."

Matt called tails and won. He kept his break weak, but it was confident enough that the red eleven rolled directly into the left pocket. "Woohoo!" Matt yelled. "Got it!"

"Nice shot," Dan said sincerely. Matt blew the next one on purpose, and Danny's four bounced off the edge of the table inches away from the right center pocket.

"Okay, let's see." Matt circled the table slowly, like he was thinking. He aimed at the fourteen and tipped it into the right corner pocket. "Startin' to get the hang of this."

"I can see that." Danny's voice was flat. Matt missed his next shot on purpose but made the next, missed again, made the next. He still played better than Danny, who kept his cool, even as his face, ears and neck flushed redder and redder. The other miners returned from the bar and circled the table closely.

"Probably beginner's luck," Matt said after he'd sunk the eight-ball. Suze ran over, and Matt put his arm around her shoulder. This night was going pretty good.

"Some luck," Danny spat. "I don't have two hundred on me."

"No sweat, man. Gimme your watch, and I'll hold on to it until you get the money."

"Fine," Danny muttered. "I can't believe this."

"Hey, he fuckin' won." Ryan butted in. "Show some goddamn respect." The miners around the table murmured in agreement.

"Are you serious? He sharked me."

"Sharked you? I ain't seen Matt play a game of pool in his fuckin' life. You lost, buddy. Beginner's luck, am I right,

Matt?" Ryan shrugged his shoulders at Danny and looked at Matt, who stood next to the pool table brushing the front of his flannel shirt like there was something to brush off. Keith appeared out of nowhere behind Matt and crossed his arms, practically growling over Matt's head. Danny ran his hand through his hair, handed Matt his watch without looking at him, and stomped toward the door.

After a brief silence, most of the remaining miners around the pool table went back to the bar to refill their glasses.

"So, where are we going to dinner?" Suze asked brightly. "I haven't been on a date in a while."

"Name the place, baby. I'm thinking Anvil Tavern for some of those fancy chicken wings. Check out this watch. He's probably gettin' that money right now." Matt waved at the pretty bartender. "Hey little lady! Round of Fireball for everybody back here."

The pretty bartender set five shot glasses on the bar and poured a round. Matt clinked his glass against Suze's and took the shot. "I'm gonna go for a smoke," he said. "I'll be right back."

"I'll be right back, too." Ryan pulled on his flannel and followed Matt out the front door and into the cool, sunlit night. "Did you really shark him?"

"The fuck does that mean?"

"Just fuckin' wondering," Ryan mumbled. Matt lit his cigarette and passed the lighter to Ryan, but Ryan had his eyes fixed over Matt's right shoulder. "Fuck. Matt. Turn the fuck around."

"What?" Matt asked. He looked over his shoulder and came face-to-face with Andy. Two of Andy's buddies from the shop stood on either side of him, arms crossed. Danny trailed behind, glowering at the whole scene. Ryan lit his cigarette.

"I heard you fuckin' sharked my cousin, asshole." Andy walked right up to Matt, so close that Matt could smell the beer sweating from his forehead.

"The fuck you talkin' about?"

"You know the fuck I'm talkin' about. Gimme that goddamn watch."

"Hell no. I fuckin' won it. Not my fault Danny-boy here sucks at pool."

"Yeah, well, you were supposed to suck at pool. You knew exactly what you were doin'."

"Are you fuckin' —" Andy wound back his fist and punched Matt in the mouth before he could finish his sentence. Matt's vision went black for a second. Something lodged in Matt's throat, and he coughed it out. It was a tooth. "Jesus fucking Christ."

Ryan reached over and put his cigarette out on Andy's jacket. It burned through the fleece in a perfect circle. "That's what I fuckin' think of your dandy-ass cousin."

Andy stared at Ryan in disbelief, then turned and socked Matt in the mouth again. Bright green lights exploded behind Matt's eyelids as his head snapped back. He fell hard on the cement, and one of Andy's guys kicked him in the ribs, then kicked him again. Sharp pain shot through Matt's torso and up through his spine; all he could do was curl himself into a ball and hope they would leave. Ryan shoved the guy, and Matt heard someone's nose break. A large hand reached down and fumbled with the watch as Matt felt another kick to his back. His legs went numb, but he didn't open his mouth for fear that he'd whimper instead of yell.

Five enormous fingers pulled the watch off Matt's wrist. "Fuckin' shark," someone spat, and another kick landed at the base of Matt's spine. Matt knew it was bad; he couldn't even react, couldn't even flinch as the toe of the man's work boot ripped through the flannel of his best shirt. He heard Danny say faintly over the roar in his ears, "Hey, cut it out! Shouldn't we get them some help?"

"Don't be a fuckin' pansy, Danny," Andy said. Matt felt a wad of spit hit the top of his neck, right behind his left ear. "He fuckin' deserved it."

second sleep

Two in the morning was Richard's favorite time of night. KNOM had retired its late-night DJs and replaced them with canned specialty hours, but even the monotony of the rotated midnight programs failed to lull Richard to a sleep deep enough to miss Nome's darkest hour. His mother had taught him that sleep comes in pairs: the first half of the night should relax the mind and conjure up mild visions as your head and heaven sort themselves out behind your tired eyelids, while the second sleep ought to be the thoughtless KO of the dead. In the middle of the night, between the twin halves of unconsciousness, one should stretch one's legs and reset one's purpose for the day so that one does not wake up aimless, for it is not written that man should arise from his bedside grave with no direction. Richard took his mother's advice to heart every morning and stretched his legs all the way to his front porch, where he could gaze into the middle distance at the other cotton-mouthed double sleepers.

On this particular night, Richard had awoken from a dream that stemmed from his lower head. He looked guiltily at his wife in the darkness and rolled his aging body away from her toward the bedroom door. He slept in his socks and managed to sneak past his sleeping grand-babies, into his boots and jacket, and out the door without stirring a soul in the house. His dog, Bubba, broke into an alert but silent trot behind him.

Two A.M. was as dark as it got in Nome any time of year, but the streetlight next to Richard's house cast a pool of bright white light on the snow that covered the road and threw thick shadows on the rooftops of the one-story houses on Richard's block. Richard's fingers closed around a loose cigarette, and he put it between his lips, not to smoke, he told himself, but to hold. Bubba huddled against his leg and whimpered. The dog just did not take well to the cold.

A pair of girls rounded the corner and stumbled past Richard's porch. They leaned on each other's shoulders, giggling, and did not look at him. Richard had seen them before, and thought these new white girls in town were a bad influence on the area youth. But they were pretty, so he credited them with at least bundling up and keeping each other company as they skated home across the icy roads. Richard knew he was an old softy when it came right down to it.

Richard's other hand found a lighter in his parka pocket, and he lit his cigarette with a muted click: the last cigarette before the second sleep. Richard closed his eyes for the first drag, and when he opened them, he saw that once again, he was not alone in the early hour. Black shadows moved between the houses on the other side of the road and spilled out onto the glimmering street. Richard counted two men — boys, Richard thought, given how skinny they were — and as they tramped toward him, one of them raised his hand in a late-night salute. Richard nodded back and turned his attention to the ashy tip of his cigarette. His dog was starting to beg in earnest, and Richard's fingers were getting cold.

Suddenly Richard perceived that the low whine in his right ear was not attributable to Bubba. He looked down at the dog huddled against his leg and then further up the road. Two white headlights shown through the black night, and the whine transformed into the engine roar of a Jeep. Richard saw that the truck was going extremely fast, too fast for the slick road, and his heart caught in his chest as the vehicle shot through the stop sign just a few houses away. Richard pulled his cigarette out of his mouth and yelled at the two black figures in the street to move. The boys leapt across the road, but one of them was less sure of his footing and fell heavily onto the ice directly in the line of the truck.

Richard could no longer hear the roar of the Jeep or the sound of his own voice, though the vibrations in his chest told him he was hollering. The truck swerved wildly to the right, but the adjustment came too late: a sickening crack broke through the late night like a gunshot as the Jeep plundered over the fallen boy's spine. Richard hadn't seen the boy's face, and now he looked away as it came into white relief in the streetlight. Richard instead concentrated on the Jeep's clear window. For an instant, he locked eyes with a woman he'd never seen before in the driver's seat. Her green eyes sparkled against her pale skin and pale hair, and her mouth dilated around a startled O, like an animal. Richard met her feral gaze in the instant the Jeep's front tires fell over the boy's body, and then she was gone. The Jeep's back axle rolled over the corpse, and, without stopping, the truck sped off into the onyx night.

the innocents

"SO, WHAT'D YOU GET FIRED FOR?" TOM stuck a new chunk of tobacco in his cheek and chewed circularly while staring at the TV screen.

Courtney closed the front door and dropped her duffel bag at her feet. Cold air rushed into the tiny living room, and she decided that her first contribution to her new home would be to build an arctic entry. The only light in the house came from the television, but even that light was enough to see that the living room was small and cluttered. "Nice to meet you too," she greeted her new roommate. "I'm Courtney."

"I know." Tom spat into the tin can in his lap. "Why'd you get fired?"

"Well, right after I ran the NL 300 I —"

"What's that?"

"Northern Lights 300. It's an Iditarod qualifier. Like a dog team race. My boss let me run his extra dogs to get some experience in case I wanted to run the Iditarod next year. So after the Northern Lights —"

"What place you come in?"

"Red lantern. At least I finished, though."

"What's red lantern mean?"

Courtney felt defeated. She could only make out half of Tom's face in the semi-faded glow of the TV screen. "Last."

"So, you got fired for coming in last?"

"No. Would you let me finish a sentence, please? I got fired because my boss brought six extra dogs to the race and didn't tell me, so I didn't ship down enough dog food. So my boss had to get more dog food when we got there, which is like, super expensive. He said it wasn't worth it to keep paying me if I was going to do stuff like that. Which is unfair, because I swear he never told me he was bringing the extra dogs. It all kind of went downhill after that. Anyway, I was living in a spare room in their guesthouse, which I obviously can't do anymore, and housing is really hard to find in the winter."

"So that's why you're livin' here."

"So that's why I'm livin' here. Can we turn on some lights?"

"Caleb okay with you bein' unemployed?"

"I'm actually not unemployed. I just got a job as an advocate at —"

"What's an advocate?"

The front door of the house opened, and Caleb stomped in, scattering snow and dirt on the living room carpet. He closed the door quickly, but now Courtney was glad for the draft; the salty, stagnant air in the house was starting to make her feel claustrophobic.

"Hey there, brother," Tom drawled. "Courtney here was just telling me what her new job's about."

"Oh yeah? Real proud of her." Caleb kissed Courtney's cheek and put his hand on her shoulder to steady himself as he untied his boots.

"Thanks!" she beamed at Caleb and turned back to Tom. "An advocate is someone who goes to court with women and children who are staying in a shelter. I get paid by Kawerak and kind of rotate around to different sites. You know, in case anybody needs someone to explain what's going on, hold their hand, make sure that they're not being ignored. Just so they know someone's on their side during the proceedings."

"This for what?"

"Um, homeless people who got evicted, domestic violence survivors, kids who can't stay in their foster care placements, mostly. But also people who show up at the hospital and need —"

"So you get paid just to hold their hand?" For the first time that night, Tom turned his attention away from the television and looked Courtney in the eye. She was momentarily frozen by how similar the blueness of Tom's gaze was to Caleb's, as if they were twins rather than brothers separated by five years and three siblings. Then

Tom, maintaining eye contact, opened his mouth and let a large, tar-filled drop of saliva fall into his cup. He cut the dark spittle off with his lips and turned back to the television.

Courtney glanced at Caleb for support, but Caleb only shook off his boots and hopped around Courtney to take a seat on the couch next to his brother. Tom passed him his chew, and Caleb took a finger-full. Caleb's eyes locked on to the TV screen. "Sometimes that's all they need," Courtney said quietly.

"Mm-hmm. Real proud of you, honey." Caleb's North Carolina drawl took on the leisurely pace of his brother's as the chew settled against his gum. "Tom, wanna bowl?"

"You got some, brother? Hell, yeah."

Courtney picked up her duffel bag and slinked past the couch. The house was one story and consisted of the living room, which barely fit the television, coffee table, and folding chair, an open kitchen, a bathroom with a stand-up shower, and a single bedroom adjacent to the living room. She opened the bedroom door and was greeted by the stench of dog shit. Courtney turned on the light, and six blind, mewling pups turned their noses her way. The puppies were sprawled inside a black crate lined with filthy newspapers. Gracie, Caleb's dog, lay on a spread of *Nome Nugget* newspapers on the floor next to her young litter. "Jesus, Caleb," she called over her shoulder. Neither man turned to look at her. "Caleb!" she said louder.

"What, hon?"

"Can't you get her to shut up?" Tom muttered.

"What?" Courtney asked.

"I said, I'm watching television."

The mewling grew more insistent. Courtney knocked on the doorframe between the living room and the bedroom. "Caleb," she said. "C'mere."

Caleb stood and ambled around the couch. Courtney pulled him into the bedroom and shut the door. "Hey, hon," Caleb said. He pulled Courtney into a firm hug. "I'm trying to spend some time with Tom. You know he's going through a rough time."

Courtney stepped back and gestured to the dogs. "Have they been in here all day? Without any light? Has anyone been in here to clean them up or feed Gracie or anything?" Gracie looked up at Courtney pitifully from her pile of newspapers.

"Tom said he'd do it. I guess he didn't, but I'm not gonna get on his case about it. He's been here for like not even a day. Gracie's fine."

"Yeah, well I've only been here for fifteen minutes. I'm so tired. Why do I have to do this?"

"Baby, you don't have to do anything. Gracie usually eats her puppies' poop. Tom will take care of it if she doesn't. I'll talk to him."

"And meanwhile I get to sleep in a room that smells like dog shit? You know I'm going to have to clean this up anyway. This isn't fair."

"Hon, you said it was okay for him to stay with us

just until he gets on his feet. I'll pick up his slack. Gracie's my dog."

"You have to make sure he actually gets on his feet, okay? Did you talk to anybody at Kawerak?"

"Yeah, I don't know what they're going to be able to do for him. He's really only ever done construction before. I think I'll have better luck with Andy at the auto shop."

Courtney felt her chin begin to tremble. "Construction! It's only February! What's he going to do all winter?"

"We'll see, we'll see. I said I'd take care of it, didn't I? Can't you talk to Christina? Maybe her brother can set him up with a gig or something."

Courtney clamped her teeth together to keep her voice steady. "Okay, fine. Get out of here, so I can clean up Gracie and the puppies. He'd better at least take her for a walk tomorrow."

"Thanks, hon. I love you."

"Love you," Courtney mumbled as Caleb shut the door.

* * *

"HEY, JANE," COURTNEY SAT DOWN NEXT TO A LITTLE GIRL drawing by herself on the living room floor of the shelter. "I'm Courtney."

The girl jumped and looked up. "Hay is for horses," she said. She glared at Courtney, then turned back to her paper. She clutched the orange marker so tightly that her fingers turned white.

"Well, hello, then," Courtney said. "Whatcha drawing there?"

"Foxes," Jane said. Courtney noticed that her dark eyes were drawn with exhaustion.

"Foxes! I love foxes! What are the foxes doing?"

"Talking," the little girl answered listlessly.

"Talking foxes! Who are they talking to?"

"Annie."

"Who's A —"

"Jane, honey, time for a snack!" Molly called from down the hall. "Peanut butter and crackers!"

Jane snapped her head toward the kitchen, and Courtney watched her face flush a deep red. "I don't want peanut butter and crackers!" she shouted. She punched her orange marker through the paper, leaving a hole where one of the fox's faces had been. "I hate peanut butter and crackers." She started to sob.

"Shh, shh," Courtney crooned. "Jane. Ja-ane. C'mere, baby. C'mere." She held out her arms and lightly rubbed Jane's shoulders. The girl turned away from the door to the hallway and crawled into Courtney's lap.

◼ ◼ ◼

Tom was smoking on the front steps of the house when Courtney got home. "Hi!" she said, still warm from the shelter. "Thanks for smoking out here. That house gets a little small, huh."

"Ain't a problem. Sorry we got such a rough start."

Tom took his cigarette out of his mouth, examined it, and pitched it into the night. The two of them watched the red ash sizzle out in the snow. "It's just that I've always been pretty protective of Caleb, and I'd hate to see him with the wrong girl. Truce?" He held out his hand.

Courtney took it. "Sure. I want the best for him too. How was your day?"

"Good, good. Waitin' for Caleb to get out of work to take me to Andy's for an interview. And I got that newspaper cleaned up, changed it, took Gracie for a walk. She's a good old bitch. What litter's she on?"

"Third. I wasn't around for the first two, though."

"Yeah, well, seems like she got tired of cleaning up after them little'uns. You think we're gonna be able to sell them?"

"Oh yeah, people love dogs around here. Caleb has a few people he wants to give them to."

"You can't just give puppies away! We can sell 'em." Tom spat into the darkness as a truck pulled around the corner. "I think this is him."

The truck stopped in front of the house, and Caleb waved at Courtney from the driver's seat. Tom brushed his hands on his parka and lumbered to the passenger side. "Wish me luck at my new job!" he called to her.

"Good luck!" she shouted over the engine. Tom slammed the door shut, and Caleb blew her a kiss as he pulled forward. Courtney waved as the truck pulled out of the driveway, then ran contentedly up the steps to her new home.

Caleb and Tom came back later that night with pizza from Milano's. "He got the job!" Caleb whooped as the men took off their boots inside the doorway and set the pizza on the table in front of the TV. "He's a workin' man now!"

"Time to celebrate!" Tom grinned. "You guys got beer?"

Caleb stiffened. "Nah, man, we don't keep that around here."

"Too bad," Tom said nonchalantly, and took a bite out of his piece of pizza.

◼ ◼ ◼

"So how's it going with Jane?" Myra asked, glancing at Courtney over Jane's file.

"I think pretty well," Courtney said, less confidently than she would have liked. Courtney had known Myra for almost two years; they'd trained for a marathon together last spring, and Courtney had even looked after Myra's dogs last summer while Myra was at camp. Courtney couldn't remember the last time she'd seen Myra inside, and had been surprised to see Myra wearing a pantsuit and makeup when she walked into the courthouse. While Myra looked natural and relaxed in her role as District Attorney, Courtney felt itchy and uncomfortable in her new clothes and the florescent lighting. She scratched her left ankle with the toe of her right boot and tried to keep her attention on Myra. She really felt most at ease around kids and dogs.

"So," Myra continued. "I know you're new. And I know you know that your main job is to keep Jane safe, but you also have to help her and her mom understand what's going on during the trial, the court process, and see if they need anything. You weren't here for the grand jury, but Jane actually did pretty great with that. I just — I hate to have to put kids on the stand if I can help it, but she's got to testify. It's your job, mostly, to help her understand that her uncle's going to be present. I've seen it where a lot of family members show up and act real hostile towards the kids when the other relatives are present, or all sit behind the defendant, which sends a message.

"Jane's mom said at the grand jury that she doesn't remember the night of the event, doesn't recall her statements to the Trooper even though we've got live audio of them, and it's really just a mess. The waiting period between the grand jury and jury trials is so long, you know, it becomes believable. She dropped the charges a while ago, but I'm sure you know that. It's a *State v. the uncle* case. Results from the nurse were inconclusive: Jane had a little swelling, but nothing obviously traumatic. Nothing that could be proven to be more than a five-year-old would normally have. How do you think Jane'll handle the stand in front of her uncle? They've sure waited long enough, right? It's been almost a year since the grand jury." Myra looked down at one of the papers spread out on her desk. "The family's come all the way from St. Michael, and the defense counsel is from Anchorage."

Courtney thought back to the tantrum Jane had thrown over the peanut butter and crackers. It had been almost three weeks since then, and Jane had become noticeably more smiley and talkative around Courtney, but she still jumped at loud sounds or when she saw movement out of the corner of her eye. She overcompensated for her nervousness by being boisterous and loud in the shelter. Some of the other moms thought Jane was a bad role model for their own children, which Courtney found hard to watch but understood. "I don't know," she told Myra. "I honestly wish I could be more confident."

"The worst thing is when a kid gets up there and testifies, and then a room full of adults doesn't believe them. You know what that does to their self-esteem? Totally shoots it. Can't let that happen to Jane, not after what she's been through already. Let's bring her in, see if she can answer a few questions with me. We did this before the grand jury, but I just want to make sure we're still on the same page, and you're here as witness for any testimony discrepancies."

"I'll get her." Courtney stood and opened the door to Myra's office. Jane and her mom were seated right outside the door, and Courtney wondered if they had heard the entire conversation. "Hey, Jane, c'mere."

"Kiss!" Jane's mom insisted. Jane kissed her mom on the cheek and hopped off her chair. Courtney held out her hand to the girl, who took it and let herself be led into the room.

"Jane, this is my friend, Myra," Courtney said once they were all seated. "You met Myra before too, remember?" Jane nodded. "You know how we're going to have to talk about what happened before you and your mom left St. Michael? Myra's going to be asking some of those questions, and she's going to help you practice answering them."

"Okay," Jane said, picking at the ends her braids.

"Nice to see you again," Myra said seriously, as if she were talking to another adult instead of a six-year-old girl.

"You too," Jane mumbled.

"Have you been having fun playing with Courtney?"

"Yeah." Jane turned and grinned at Courtney, who beamed back.

"Well, that's great! Remember when we talked about the difference between a truth and a lie? Has Courtney been talking to you about that too?"

"Yeah! Truth is something that's real. A lie is something that's not real."

"Excellent. So, what if I said you were nine years old? Would that be a truth or a lie?"

"Lie!"

"Exactly! And what if I said you're in first grade now?"

"True!"

"Good, good. Okay, so has Courtney told you about what's happening next week?"

Jane looked at Courtney with huge eyes. "Uncle's going to jail." Courtney glanced at Myra and shook her head slightly. She'd never told Jane that.

Myra smiled. "Well, maybe not. First you, your mom, and your uncle have to answer a few questions about why you and your mom moved to Nome. Do you remember what happened before you came to Nome?"

"Yeah."

"Great. Can you tell me about it again?"

"Yeah."

"Okay, good. Remember, we only want truths here, okay?"

"Okay."

"So, what happened?"

"Uncle came home. We were sleeping in my auntie's living room, and he was really loud. He came into the living room where we were sleeping." Jane looked down at her pink boots.

"Great, you're doing great. What did he do in the living room?"

"He tried to take off my nightie, and he put his hand on my pee-pee."

"And then what?"

"Then Mom woke up and started yelling and everyone woke up and she called Mike and we had to get on an airplane and go to Nome." Jane's face scrunched, and she closed her eyes tightly.

"Jane, thank you for sharing that with Courtney and me. Do you think you can share that with a few other people next week?"

Jane nodded, eyes still closed.

"Excellent. You did so great last time, and I know you're going to be fantastic next week. But only truths, remember? What did you do when your uncle put his hand on your pee-pee?"

"I said, 'Stop! I'm sleeping.'"

"Thank you for sharing that with me. Courtney's going to be asking you a few more questions over the next week, so you're going to be really prepared. Do you want to know exactly how it's going to work?" Jane nodded again. "Good. Let's take a little walk, so you can see where you'll be sitting." Myra stood up, and Jane and Courtney followed her lead out of the office. "We get to go through a special door because we're going to be the ones doing the talking. Isn't that cool?"

"Yeah!" Jane shouted. Courtney could tell that Jane was acting up because she was tired, and hoped that the interview wouldn't take too much longer.

"Hey, we're just going to take a look at the courtroom," Courtney told Jane's mom. Jane waved, and her mom waved back.

"Who's Mike?" Courtney asked as she and Myra followed Jane through the courthouse hallway.

"Village Police Officer. VPO." Myra frowned at the confusion on Courtney's face. "Like, local police. They didn't teach you this in training? How long have you been here? You still haven't been out to any of the villages?"

"Only the villages that are race checkpoints," Courtney said. Myra sighed.

They opened the side door to the courtroom.

"So," Myra said to Jane, "this is where we'll be next week." The courtroom was aggressively bright, with paper-white walls and blond wooden benches.

"This is like church!" Jane said. She let go of Courtney's hand and ran up to the judge's bench to surveil the room.

"Yeah, exactly! And you're gonna be right where the minister would give his sermon." Myra patted the edge of the witness stand. "Jane, c'mere for a second. You're gonna sit or stand here, whatever makes you feel most comfortable, and answer my questions with only truths."

Jane skipped up to Myra and solemnly put her hands on either side of the stand. "Only truths," she said.

"Yes, only truths. There are going to be twelve people sitting over here, on these pews" — Myra gestured to the jury benches — "and some people are going to be out in those pews, too, just like at church. And then there's going to be a judge here, and he's in charge. He's like the teacher, so you have to do what he says, no matter what. Right?"

"Right!" Jane said, bouncing on the tips of her toes.

"And then your uncle's going to be here," Myra said, pointing to the defense table. "This isn't going to be like last time. There are going to be a lot more people here, including your uncle, but I need you to keep telling truths, okay? Whenever you're up here, you need to tell only truths."

Jane nodded.

"And I'm going to be here." Myra gestured to the table directly in front of Jane. "I'm going to ask you questions, just like we did today, and you're going to tell me only truths, got it?" Jane nodded again. "Then maybe your uncle's lawyer will ask you some questions after me, and you have to tell him only truths, too. Right?"

"Right!"

"Awesome. High five, Jane." Jane jumped to reach Myra's hand, and the two grinned at each other. "Alright, let's get you back to your mom."

"Okay!" Jane hopped down from the witness stand and raced to the courtroom door. Myra and Courtney followed behind.

"She's going to do great," Myra said warmly. "I'm really confident. You've been doing a great job with her. Pretty amazing, actually, compared to a lot of other kids."

"Thanks!" Courtney smiled. "I really like working with her."

"Do you think you'll be an advocate for a while?"

"I hope so! Maybe I'll go back to school and come back to Nome."

"Well, that would be great. We need some consistency. All the turnover is bad for the kids, especially because these court dates are so spread out. We want to make everything easy for them. If you need anything like a recommendation, just let me know."

"Thank you! I will. And I'll call you if I have any questions."

"Good. I'll see you next week."

⊞ ⊞ ⊞

COURTNEY PULLED HER BOOTS OFF AT THE FRONT DOOR AND surveyed the scene in the tiny house: Tom slumped on the couch, his head lolled back, Gracie curled up next to him, the rambling TV set, a beer on the side table. Courtney walked directly through the living room and into the bedroom. Inside, the puppies cried quietly. She closed the door and started to clean up their poop, which was noticeably more substantial than it had been when she first moved in.

Caleb came home less than five minutes later. "What the fuck?" Courtney heard him say in the living room. "What the fuck is this, Tom?"

Tom grunted awake and mumbled something.

"Get your shit together, man. You're gonna be a father. A father. You're gonna have a little girl. You can't be doin' this. Did you go to work?"

Silence.

"You gotta be kidding me. They're gonna fire your ass, and then you're not even gonna be able to make it back to see your kid."

Caleb flung the bedroom door open. "Jesus, Courtney, I didn't know you were in here. God, it stinks." Caleb knelt to clean up the newspaper in the crate. "Woah, look at this. I think one of these little guys died."

Tom appeared in the doorway. "Don't you talk to me like that."

"Go back to sleep, Tom," Caleb said quietly, still bent over the crate. "Courtney, I don't think this one's breathing. What do you think?" he held up a limp little body in his right hand. Courtney took the puppy from Caleb. It was cold.

"Don't you tell me what to do!" Tom aimed a kick at Caleb's back and Caleb fell forward, catching himself on the crate. The puppies whimpered.

"What the fuck?" Caleb stood up to face Tom. "Did you just kick me?"

Tom was silent, but didn't move.

"Don't you ever do that again," Caleb said quietly. "I didn't bring you here so you could lose your job. Don't you touch me, and don't you ever, ever touch her," Caleb pointed to Courtney. Tom looked at Courtney too, as if he'd suddenly gotten an idea.

███

"So, how's it going with them?" Molly asked Courtney after everyone in the shelter had gone to bed.

"I think okay. Jane seems to really like Myra, and she's been a little calmer here, so I think she'll be fine at trial."

"Yeah. Want coffee?" Courtney nodded. Molly continued, "It's a tough situation."

Courtney waited as Molly washed out the coffee pot.

"Jane and her mom really — I mean, they really rely on Jane's uncle and his family," Molly said. "They were living with them. Jane's dad, my cousin, he left pretty soon after Jane was born. Her mom doesn't have income and doesn't practice subsistence. Her brother does all the hunting, fishing, everything. We've been doing the best we can to feed them here, but if they leave —" Molly poured more beans into the restaurant-sized coffee grinder. "I remember what it was like to be completely dependent on someone. Even for my housing." She glanced discreetly at Courtney.

"Yeah, it's tough," Courtney admitted. "Caleb's brother is still living with us, and he's having some troubles."

"Caleb. At Kawerak, right?"

"Yeah. He's an environmental specialist over there."

"Good job. Sounds like a good man." Molly took two mugs down from a cabinet.

"Well, his brother's a mess," Courtney volunteered. "He's got some problems with alcohol, his ex-girlfriend, who's back in South Carolina, is going to have a baby real soon, and he doesn't have any money, and he kind of kicks Caleb around. Like he actually kicked him the other day."

Molly raised an eyebrow over her wire-rimmed glasses. "Well, if you ever feel threatened, even if he's not directly hurting you, you can stay here. You know you're welcome."

"Thanks, Molly. I hope it doesn't come to that."

"Me, too." Molly shook the grounds into the coffee maker. "You take cream?"

■ ■ ■

"I'M A DADDY!" TOM SHOUTED AS SOON AS COURTNEY OPENED the door to the house. He and Caleb were seated on the couch in front of an enormous vanilla birthday cake. "Baby girl! Her name's Kiley!" He held out his phone to show Courtney a photo of a wrinkled, frowning newborn.

"She's beautiful!" Courtney exclaimed.

"She is, isn't she? Want some cake?"

"Thanks! This is great!"

"Caleb picked it up," Tom said affectionately, mussing up Caleb's hair. "Best little brother ever." Gracie wagged her tail and licked Courtney's hand.

※ ※ ※

ON THE MORNING OF THE TRIAL, COURTNEY DROVE CALEB'S truck to the shelter. The pre-dawn sky cast a cerulean glow on the snow, the truck, and Courtney's hands on the steering wheel.

"How you doin' today, lady?" Courtney enthused when Jane hopped into the back seat of the truck. "You got your coloring book all set?"

"Yeah!"

"How's it going?" Courtney asked Jane's mom.

"Good, good," Jane's mom said wearily.

"Everyone have breakfast?" Jane's mom nodded. Jane looked at her feet. "Great," Courtney said lightly. "Jane, I have some cereal for you in the car if you want it. I also have some grilled cheese sandwiches for lunch, and some chips. What do you want for dinner, Jane?"

"Um, I don't know," Jane said.

"How about pizza?" Courtney asked, determinedly cheerful.

"Okay," Jane whispered.

"Whatever you want, lady. You get to be all bossy today." Courtney glanced at Jane in the rearview mirror and saw that Jane was smiling quietly into her coloring book. "Okay?" she asked.

"Okay," Jane agreed.

Courtney drove slowly through town, keeping an eye out for people walking on the side of the road in the blue light. They didn't pass any cars.

"Alright, we're here." Courtney pulled into a space on Front Street right across from the court house. "Ready to go?" Jane waddled out of the truck in her pink snowsuit, her arms sticking out comically from her sides. Her mom took her hand, and they walked together ahead of Courtney through the post office door and back to the courthouse.

Courtney found Myra and shook hands with the State Trooper who had handled the case. Myra guided Jane's mother to a separate office, and Courtney settled down with Jane outside the courtroom to work on the coloring book until the first recess.

"Hey, Jane," Myra said soberly at the break as she sat down next to them. "I need to talk to Courtney for a second, okay? We'll just be right here." The two women slid further down the bench, away from the little girl. "Hey," Myra said quietly, "don't tell Jane any of this, obviously, but her mother denied saying anything she told the Trooper again." Myra put her hand on Courtney's shoulder. "How's it going out here?"

"Good, good. We're just coloring."

"You're keeping her really calm. That's great. I think she's going to have to testify in about half an hour. The clerk will come get you."

"Thanks, Myra."

"Alright. I'm going to head back in."

"Jane! How about we make some paper plate angels?" Courtney took some paper plates out of her bag and started sketching the outline of a woman.

"Woah!" Jane set her coloring book aside and grabbed the plate from Courtney.

The clerk opened the door twenty minutes later. "Ready?" he asked.

Jane jumped, then recovered herself. "Ready!" she yelled. She threw down her marker and stood up, then looked back at Courtney. Courtney smiled back reassuringly and ushered her after the clerk.

"Jane, I am so proud of you," Courtney said. "Go out there and tell Myra some truths. I'll be right here with the door open so you can see me."

"Okay!" The clerk waved Jane up to the witness stand. Courtney leaned against the door. From her vantage point, Jane's tiny frame was dwarfed by the judge's bench. Myra stood directly in front of Jane, and the Trooper sat behind the prosecution table. Another lawyer in a gray suit and a man that Courtney assumed was Jane's uncle sat behind the table for the defense. Courtney couldn't see the jury.

"Jane," Jane responded to a question Courtney didn't hear. She caught Jane's eye and smiled. "J-A-N-E."

"And Jane, how old are you?" Myra asked.

"Six."

"Your Honor, I would like to forgo reciting the oath due to age."

"Proceed."

"Jane, do you know the difference between a truth and a lie?"

"Yes."

"Can you please tell us what that is?"

"A truth is something that really happened, and a lie is something that didn't happen and isn't real."

"Good. So I need you to tell me and everyone here in this room the truth for every single question we ask, okay?"

"Okay."

The defense rose. "Objection."

"Overruled," said the judge. "The witness is considered under oath."

Myra nodded. "Jane, can you please point to your uncle?"

Jane pointed.

"And what was the last thing that your uncle did before you left his house in St. Michael?"

"Objection."

Jane started to bounce on her toes as the testimony went on. Courtney wanted to go out and quiet her. She looked hungry. Between objections, Jane managed to tell her story exactly as she had described it to Myra and Courtney. Courtney leaned against the doorway and nodded along with each answer, more aware of how Jane looked than what she was saying. She hadn't realized that trials were so long, and hoped that the questioning would be over soon.

Suddenly Jane stopped bouncing. She sighed dramatically on the stand. "Then me and Mom flew to Nome and I met Annie, who can talk to foxes."

Courtney stood up straight. Myra's smile tightened. "Okay," Myra said. "Thank you, Jane. No more questions."

"The defense would like to question the witness," the lawyer at the defense table said. Myra looked at him sharply.

"Go ahead," said the judge.

"Jane," the lawyer began, standing up to approach the witness stand. "What do you mean, you met Annie, who can talk to foxes?"

"She couldn't talk to people, but she could talk to foxes."

"Did the foxes talk back?"

"Uh-huh. I didn't understand them."

The lawyer nodded solemnly. "Did your uncle often get you ready for bed?"

Myra cut in. "Objection."

"Overruled."

"Sometimes," Jane said.

"Uh-huh. And did he ever give you baths?"

Myra rose. "Objection."

"Overruled."

"When I was little, but now I take my own showers."

"And did you ever feel scared when he gave you a bath or got you ready for bed?"

"No."

"Did he ever hurt you when he gave you a bath?"

"Objection."

"Sustained."

"No," Jane said.

"Okay, thank you, Jane." The lawyer turned to the judge. "No more questions."

"Thank you, Jane," the judge said. "You can head on out, now."

Jane jumped back from the witness stand and ran into Courtney's arms.

※ ※ ※

"What the hell was that?" Myra asked Courtney at the next recess. "Has she ever said anything like that to you before? Why didn't you tell me?"

"No, I mean, when I first started she was drawing foxes, but I didn't think —" Courtney sputtered. "I'm sorry. I didn't know. Seriously, Myra. Is it a big deal?"

"Well, it does discredit her a little bit. Reminded the jury that kids use their imaginations, which is not great. And this jury's all from Nome, no one's from St. Michael, so it's not clear how they'll go. I'll send a note to the defense, and you were a witness when she recounted her story to me, so I'll talk to you about next steps. That'll probably be tomorrow."

"I'm sorry."

"If it didn't come up as an issue before the trial, it's not your fault. Hopefully it won't matter one way or another.

Defense is almost done talking about the uncle's character et cetera."

Courtney looked at the ground. "What do you think's gonna happen?"

"Well, the family really needs him. The defense is persuasive. I'll let you know. Just keep doing what you've been doing."

"Can I take Jane to get some dinner? Do we have to stay here?"

"Sure, take her out. But come back before five." Myra ran her hand over her short hair, smoothing it back from her forehead. She sighed heavily and walked back into the courtroom.

"Can you tell me more about Annie?" Courtney asked Jane over an untouched pizza at Milano's, the high-boothed restaurant across from the courthouse.

"Um, she was really little. Like my cousin. I only saw her for one night and then she left." Jane held her piece of pizza in front of her face so Courtney couldn't see her expression.

"What happened with the foxes?"

"She didn't talk right to me or Mom or Auntie Molly, but the foxes barked at her, and she barked back. It was cool."

"That's it?"

"Yeah, then Auntie Molly made us go back to bed."

"Do you know what happened to her?"

"She went home. I miss her."

The trial ended at five o'clock exactly, and the jurors and observers spilled out of the courtroom in a mute wave. Courtney recognized several people from around town, and a few gave her tight smiles. Myra and the State Trooper were the last ones to come through the brown double doors of the courtroom. "Hi, Jane!" Myra said, forcedly cheerful. She stooped down to greet the girl at eye-level. Jane stared back at her. "I'm gonna go get your mom, okay?"

"Okay," Jane said. She rubbed her eyes.

Myra stood and returned a few minutes later, silently leading Jane's mother. Jane ran to give her a hug. Her mother held Jane's shoulders limply.

"What happened?" Courtney asked.

"They went ahead with it. Said the discrepancies in Jane's testimony weren't substantively related to the event. Jury found him guilty of harassment, which is a misdemeanor, not a felony. You won't have to give your statement," Myra said. "Sentenced to ninety days in rehab."

"That's it?" Courtney felt like she was going to cry.

Myra ignored her question. "What a day. Really not her fault at all. Plenty of elements working in this case. You would not believe. You should take them back. They look exhausted."

"Thanks, Myra."

Myra shook her head. "Yeah." She recovered herself and squatted down to talk to Jane again. "Nice to meet you!" she said. "You are such a strong and smart girl. I can't wait to see what you do next!" She straightened and shook Jane's mother's hand, then made her way over to the lawyer in the gray suit, who was standing across the hallway.

Courtney turned back to Jane and her mom and tried to smile. "Alright, who wants some ice cream?"

⁂

A late-winter evening chill had settled over Nome by the time Courtney walked back to her house. She could hear the television through the closed door. She hoped that Caleb was home, but, to her disappointment, only Tom was sitting on the couch. He looked up at her with red eyes.

"Caleb here?" she asked.

"No," Tom growled. He jerked his head back to the TV. "He's not here."

"Okay, thanks. Are you okay?"

Tom turned toward her with the same abrupt motion. "No, I'm not fuckin' okay. I'm not gonna get to see the baby." He widened his eyes and drew his mouth forward alarmingly, tensing the tendons in his neck. Courtney took a step back. "I ain't never gonna see her. My baby." His face suddenly went slack, and he slumped against the back of the couch. His head lolled onto his shoulder.

Courtney ran to the bedroom without taking her coat or boots off. The stench of dog shit, laced with something rancid, hit her as soon as she opened the bedroom door. Courtney had smelled worse during her time as a dog handler, but she gagged involuntarily. She turned on the light.

The first thing Courtney saw was Gracie. The dog lay with her head on her paws, facing away from the doorway, and didn't move as Courtney stepped into the room. Her puppies lay scattered around her, not in their kennel like they usually were. Instead of mewling, they lay still and silent. Courtney bent to examine the pup closest to the door and saw that jagged points of its skull pushed out unevenly from under its thin scalp. Without picking the puppy up, Courtney prodded lightly at one of the edges. The crown of the pup's head collapsed under her fingertip. Gracie hadn't moved. The only sound in the house was the low babbling of the television set.

Courtney stood. She was sweating. She nudged Gracie with her boot, and when the dog still didn't respond, Courtney walked out of the bedroom and straight out the front door of the house without pausing to look at Tom. She pulled her gloves out of her pockets as she slid down the middle of the slick Nome streets and jammed them onto her hands, trying to scrub the touch of the puppy's fur off her fingers. She would have run except for the weight of her bunny boots, so she shuffled along as quickly as she could, looking away from the driver's seats of the few cars that passed her.

The shelter light was on. Courtney rang the bell and waited for Molly to answer. When the older woman appeared at the door, Courtney held out her hands. "I have to stay here for a while," she said. Molly sighed quietly and opened the door wide to let her in.

jenna escapes

SPINDLY RAYS FROM THE LOW YELLOW sun glanced off the heavy floor of sea ice, blinding Jenna as she surveyed the cape. It was early afternoon, but the sun hadn't decided to set just yet; she would see its face for at least another hour. She hoped she wouldn't see anyone else. Her mother had been leaving her alone in the house more and more often now that she was getting older. On this particular occasion, she knew that her mother's church auction wouldn't end until after dinnertime because her mother had left a cup of instant ramen, a bag of Doritos, and a leftover chicken wing for Jenna to heat up while she was out. Her mother had never imagined that Jenna would venture out on her own — they'd talked about it so many times — but Jenna had been practicing maneuvering through her family's treacherous yard for several weeks to prepare for this adventure. The recent snow had been a hindrance, but Jenna had managed. And now, unbelievably, she was alone in the middle of the Bering Sea.

The wind had picked up overnight, and snow blew over the surface of the ice like desert sand. Jenna held her hand low to the ground and let the small frozen flakes crackle against her glove as they passed, leaving teardrops on her fingertips.

Jenna straightened and reached into her bag to find the kite. She pulled out the large, folded triangle of red fabric and began to open it, carefully unraveling the black cords that kept the structure together. She pulled at the ropes to test their strength, still incredulous that the thin lines could support her weight. When George had shown her how to use the kite, she had been sure that the ropes would tear and snap away from her, leaving her grounded and slow again. George had assured her that the kite was strong enough to pull a grown person on a sled up a mountain, and, under his gentle tutelage, she had learned to trust it. She had allowed the enormous red kite to fully open against the golden sky and had leaned back against the black cords, letting the wind carry her forward faster than she had ever moved in her entire life. They had practiced last summer on the softball field, and she had imagined she had just hit a homerun and was running the bases so fast that she could take off from the grass and launch into the sky. George had run behind her and caught her just as she thought she would never be able to stop. She knew she would be able to travel even faster over the slick, ice-covered cape.

The sun inched toward the horizon as Jenna began to assemble the kite. The thick red fabric was unwieldy, and she had to concentrate to keep from dropping the kite onto the ice. She remembered the way George had fastened each black buckle and tightened each knot in the cord twice over to keep her safe. Now George was gone, but she could feel his fingers working alongside hers as she filtered the fabric through her own small hands. He had been a repairman, always trying to fix things that were broken. He had known how to tie fifty different kinds of knots, had patched up the pipes in her house when they burst from the cold, and had even set a splint in her younger sister's arm when she'd crashed her snow machine last winter. No matter how hard George tried, though, he could not fix Jenna. He had worked on her for years but had given up. All she had left was his kite.

Shouting made Jenna turn around; a group of kids had climbed over the sea wall and were slipping down the snow-covered beach toward the ice. Jenna hoped that none of them would recognize her or wonder what she was doing out by herself. But when they hit the sea, the kids started to skate west, concentrating hard to avoid getting knocked over by the wind and snow. Jenna turned back to the kite.

The lonely cape stretched out in front of Jenna like the rest of her lonely life. The expanse both terrified and excited her so that her hands began to shake if she let herself think about the distance she was about to travel. She focused on working the rope to keep steady. She needed the sun's light to assemble the kite, and the afternoon was wearing on.

Jenna clipped the rope to the body of the kite and held the red fabric just above her head so that it ballooned in the wind. When the kite grew taut, it pulled her forward a few inches before her arms got tired. Perfect. Her mother would be so proud of her for doing something by herself. She turned back to look at Nome. She couldn't see her house, but the steeple of her mother's church on the other side of town stood tall against the tundra. The houses that lined the coast had their windows sealed and curtains drawn to keep out the cold. The last face she would see would be the sun's.

Jenna inspected the ropes. They looked exactly as they had when George had fastened them, so she knew that they would hold. She only had one chance to configure the kite correctly; if it got away from her, she would never be able to catch it, and then she would be stranded out on the ice, too tired to pull herself back to her house. The Bering Sea already wavered in front of her eyes.

Jenna rested for a moment and tried to think of nothing. Translucent waves of snow turned from white to navy as they crashed on the ice toward the blushing sun. Finally Jenna's vision cleared. Her arms felt strong as she lifted the ropes and fastened them, one by one, to the handles of her wheelchair. The kite would guide the wheelchair farther than she would ever be able to push it, and her sister had told her the open ocean was only a mile or two out from shore. She wondered if she would freeze or drown first. Either way, she'd see George in heaven soon.

Jenna took a deep breath and held the kite over her head. The wind snatched at it immediately, and she strained to keep hold of the red fabric. She stared into the deepening sky and silently asked her mother to forgive her. Then she let go.

The kite billowed above her, then caught a higher wind current and whisked tightly upward. It flew above the sun, and the chained wheels of Jenna's chair caught on the ice and began to roll. The cape streamed by as the kite strained and pulled, and the wind ran through Jenna's hair faster and faster. Soon she lost track of how far away from town she must be and how close she might be to the open water.

The sun had fallen halfway below the horizon by the time Jenna saw the dark blue sea. Soon, she thought, I'll really be flying.

taboo

THE SKY SHOOK AS THE MAMMOTHS thundered across the horizon, ears flapping in terror as they fled the men who hunted them through the clouds. The wind dispersed the shouts between the small, concentrated bands of hunters, but the men's footsteps were lost in the commotion of the stampede. A sharp inhale cut through the air as the men drew back their spears for the kill. A pause, and then the breathy release of twenty javelins aimed at the same mark, followed by a beat and then the crash of a mammoth body succumbing to gravity as the rest of the animals ran on steadily down to the earth from the sky. The permafrost rumbled at the impact of the massive dead animal and almost broke as the rest of the elephantine bodies collided with the tundra seconds later, but barely registered the light descent of the men who would go on to shape and live on the land long after the last mammoth disappeared from this world.

Nick sat back in his chair and sighed happily. The panicked herd, flying spears, and plunging mammoth body, mixed precisely with the elder's faint but level voice, resounded in his headphones as he watched the sound waves diminish on his computer screen. Nick had worked on the audio effects for this piece for weeks after rediscovering the Inupiaq narration in the KNOM Radio archives, untouched since its original recording. Early in the project, he had convinced his friend Morris to come to the station for an afternoon to translate the story for him from Inupiaq to English, marking each plot detail directly onto the remastered audio so he would know where to insert the effects that would enliven the story for a radio audience. He'd heard this story before, in different forms, but Nick was drawn to the homey ambiance of this recording, the hushed commentary of the listeners, the elder's smoky laugh. Nick knew the kids in Nome and the surrounding villages would love the new rendition — the more sound effects, the better for them — but he also made sure to save the original recording in the digital archives where it could be accessed by request. Tomorrow he would play the story for Morris to make sure that he had correctly timed the effects, that the mammoth herd was not stampeding over the elder's description of the first men or the calm, silver lake of the sky. Nick was ashamed that, although he had lived in Nome for over half a decade, he did not know more than a few words of Inupiaq.

Nick inserted the show's closing bed, reviewed the fadeout, counted down the last three seconds of audio, hit Save, and closed his laptop. It was late fall, and he imagined people listening to this ancient chase while navigating the icy roads on their way back from their last days at camp for the season. That people in this part of the world came from the sky made sense: the only two modern points of entry to Nome were the sky or the sea, and the sea was treacherous and unreliable as it froze and thawed and pushed and pulled the ice toward shore. He wondered if the hunters were surprised at their own weight once they hit the earth, at the drumbeat of their running feet on the land, and at the mass of the animals they chased. The elder had left these particular details out.

Nick found his immediate surroundings both quiet and idiosyncratic once he finished producing the Inupiaq, Yup'ik, or Inuit story that aired on KNOM every week. He missed the tempo of the created worlds and the old worlds: the slither and splash of the sea monsters off the arctic coasts (two, one), the gruff bellowing of the talking bears (one, one, one), the whistling and barking of the flying sled dog teams (five, four, three, two, one). Sound spun Nick's imagination into a detailed tapestry of marriages, sorcery, births, magic, kidnappings, and journeys on the tundra, all perfectly synchronized, all neatly managed. No natural sounds were ever as melodic as the audio he mixed for the radio station. Outside the theater of

Nick's headphones, any rhythm he tried to count faltered after just a few beats.

The desk phone rang. "Let's get a beer after your shift," Dave said at the other end of the line. From the echo in Dave's voice, Nick could tell that Dave was in his office bathroom. "Meet you at Breakers. Bye." The phone clicked, and Nick put down the receiver before the hollow metallic dial tone could come on.

Nick glanced at the clock. He was hungry, but it was only four in the afternoon, and he always ate his peanut butter sandwich at five. Through the window next to his second-floor desk, he could see the lights on Front Street glow in the dark afternoon. Nick stood, stretched, and went downstairs to the station kitchen to get some coffee before his DJ shift. The first winter he'd spent in Alaska, Nick had only drunk coffee at eight o'clock every morning, no matter what time the sun or his body told him it was; this had been one of the ways he could tell the difference between night and day in a land that didn't care to distinguish the hours. After several arctic winters, though, Nick had given in to his addiction and added a second cup of coffee, at four o'clock, to his routine. Coffee, Nick justified, was among the most benign coping mechanisms for the persistent winter darkness.

Nick replaced the decanter and strode into Studio A. The mic was live, so Nick waited for the mid-afternoon DJ to finish her show before speaking. "Hey," he said. "How's it going?"

"Just swell. And you?" The mid-afternoon DJ was the shortest, skinniest woman Nick had ever met, but her voice boomed into the mic like a timpani drum and only slightly softened when she was speaking to someone who was in the room with her.

"Fine, thank you. Have a good night. See you tomorrow."

"See you in the morning," the mid-afternoon DJ agreed, handing her headphones to Nick. Nick waited until she had gone back to her desk upstairs before he began his pre-show routine. He glanced at himself in the glass, rolled back his shoulders, then lightly touched the master channels, feeling the board under the first three fingertips of his right hand without altering the mix (three, two, one). At exactly two minutes past the top of the hour he flexed his jaw and announced the station ID: "You're listening to KNOM, 780 AM, 96.1 FM. It's unofficially three degrees at four-oh-two P.M. We're KNOM, yours for Western Alaska." Cue the Beach Boys singing about the summer surf. Nick winced and wished he'd gone over his pre-selected track list before he'd started his shift to catch that error; there wouldn't be any kind of surf in the Bering Sea for another six months at least.

Nick quickly checked the rest of his set, then sat back to let the Beach Boys play. He typically didn't have a lot of time to work in any of his own material during his DJ shift, so he never prepared much for his three hours on air. KNOM was hosted live sixteen hours a day to accommodate the dozens of requests, announcements, and news stories its listeners called in from Nome and the surrounding villages, but people particularly liked to use Nick's time slot to get messages out to relatives, send birthday greetings, or advertise events happening later that evening. Sometimes, in the darkest and lightest months, people called the station just to ask what time it was.

The Beach Boys had just hit their final note and given way to "Paradise City" when the phone rang. "Nick," said an elderly voice, "tell my Sonny boy that I'm making salmon with mayonnaise and cheese tonight."

"I'll get that message on the air for you, Mrs. Smith," Nick assured her in his deep, professional DJ voice. "What time is dinner?"

"Oh, around six o'clock," Mrs. Smith said. Nick knew that dinner at the Smith house was always at six, but he always asked anyway.

"I'll be sure to let him know. Have a nice day now."

"Buh-bye," Mrs. Smith said, and the line clicked.

Nick put the receiver down. Sonny had to be reminded of dinner more frequently these days. That dinner announcement told Sonny, and everyone else in Nome, to make it home by six or else.

Nick faded down Guns N' Roses (three, two, one) and faded the mic back up. "Winter has made it here to Western Alaska — a perfect opportunity to keep warm and relax inside with friends and family. We started off the hour with a little bit of paradise: the Beach Boys brought us some sunshine and Guns N' Roses followed up with 'Paradise City.' Sonny, if you're listening, your mom wants you to know that she's making salmon with mayonnaise and cheese, and dinner's at six o'clock. You're listening to *Nick in the Afternoon* — give me a call, and I'll get your message out. I'll be here until seven. Now we'll cool off a little bit with The Neighbourhood — it's 'Sweater Weather' after the break."

The news that day was evergreen: a new oceanic study concluded that the erosion of the Alaskan coastline would soon displace some of the Native villages in the Bering Straits region, someone had submitted a roundup of upcoming holiday pageants in St. Michael and Unalakleet, and *Alaska Dispatch News* had released predictions about the conditions for the Iron Dog snow machine race, which wouldn't take place for another few months. Nick tried to compensate for the news and the darkness with hard rock and inspirational pop. As one of the few radio stations in Western Alaska, KNOM generalized its music selection: there wasn't a station devoted exclusively to R&B, oldies, or Top 40, so the KNOM DJs played every genre gladly, if somewhat haphazardly. Nick lined up the pencils next to the phone, then rearranged them, then rearranged them again, perfectly this time, he was sure of it, during each song.

After three hours, Nick announced the end-of-the-hour station ID — "You're listening to KNOM, AM and FM in Nome; it's seven o'clock" — and greeted Shannon, the volunteer Tuesday night DJ. Shannon, a local woman with an impressive collection of band t-shirts, had been volunteering as the Tuesday night DJ at KNOM longer than Nick had worked at the station. She was the most popular DJ they had.

Nick washed his coffee cup in the sink and scrubbed his hands with dish soap, then pulled on his parka, gloves, hat, and scarf. Shannon was bobbing her head with her eyes closed and didn't notice Nick slip past the studio on his way out the door. He checked his pockets to make sure he had his keys, wallet, and cellphone (three, two, one). The wind slapped at Nick's face as he pushed the station door open, and Nick winced as a gust shot hardened snow up toward his chin. When Nick finally took a breath, the air was so clear that it seeped through his scarf and crystallized in the back of his throat. He shuffled across the frozen roads, past the stripped-down snow machines and the snow-covered porches, to Front Street.

Breakers was warm and warmly-lit, much more homey than Nick's tiny standalone house. Nome was starting to empty out for the winter, as most of the gold miners migrated south to find seasonal jobs in Anchorage, Washington, and Oregon before heading back up to mine when the Bering Sea thawed in the spring. The miners who stayed in Nome through the winter were some of the gnarliest men Nick had ever met: they either dove under the ice to mine or were too broke to get on a plane back to Anchorage and camped along the beach or in community housing in subzero temperatures. They were always friendly to him, though, and always surprised when they learned he'd been in the army; they didn't think he seemed tough enough. A couple women huddled together near the pool tables, not looking at anybody.

"Hey, man," Dave said as Nick slid onto the stool next to him. Dave was still in his winter coat and boots despite the body heat of the bar, his enormous shoulders rounded over his pint. Dave's bear-like physique had softened since his own stint in the army. When Nick had first moved to Nome, Dave had taken him straight to the VFW for a drink to talk about the glory days. "Good set tonight," he said now.

"You go to the bathroom more often than usual this afternoon?" Nick asked. Dave only ever listened to KNOM when he was on the toilet.

"Ate some leftover pizza last night. Excellent motivational music, man."

The bartender set an Alaskan White in front of Nick without taking his order. Nick took a sip and felt his chest unclench.

"Hey, I have some leftover moose and caribou from last season — gotta clean out my freezer. Want any of it?"

"That'd be great."

"No problem. I worry about your skinny ass. You'll finally freeze to death this winter, I can feel it. Just get me some salmon in the spring, and we'll call it even. How's your skinny ass ever gonna get laid?"

Nick sat up a little taller. "Too soon, man."

"Yeah, sorry. That's what you get for falling in love here, though: everybody leaves. Have you heard from her?"

"Nope." The last woman Nick had dated had come to Nome as a dentist for the Indian Health Service. She'd been in town for a few years, but, like so many others, had left suddenly, leaving a swath of confused patients and betrayed friends in her wake.

"Too bad, man. Maybe your cell's dead. You know how Lacey and I lost touch? She said I only responded to like a fourth of her texts when I'd actually responded to every single text I'd gotten from her? Service up here fucking sucks." Dave took a reflective swig of beer. "That wasn't going to work out anyway, though."

"No," Nick agreed. He took a napkin from the stand next to him and placed his beer in the center of the white rectangle. The ring of sweat that the bottle had left on the counter soaked through the napkin's edge, ruining the symmetry. "So why're you hiding out in the bathroom at work?"

Dave shook his head. "Fucking disaster. I can't keep doing this much longer. I got this new little girl in my caseload. She's living with relatives in town and real jumpy. You know what's so fucked up? Her uncle — she was like, five at the time — put his hands down her pants, and she started telling Myra that foxes could talk during the trial. Like in front of the judge. Myra hadn't heard anything about it before, thinks maybe that advocate — you know Courtney, right? Kind of a weird girl? — didn't catch it. Blew the whole case, the perv got some kind of misdemeanor charge. They only sent the guy to alcohol rehab, and he's already out, and now that little girl is afraid of her own shadow. And I'm gonna have to deal with that guy for the next twenty years. He'll do it again. You watch."

"Talking foxes? That's what's finally doing it?" Nick asked. Dave's moods made him anxious.

Dave refused to be baited. "Nah, man. I'd eat those things for dinner if they didn't taste so nasty. I meant the abuse. That shit's hard to handle on the daily. I'm burnin' out, man. Kawerak can't pay me enough to deal with this anymore."

Nick was quiet.

"Took me longer than most, I guess," Dave continued. "You know I've already started planning what kind of car I'm going to get when I can buy one that won't be automatically covered in shit as soon as it hits the road? I got a list." He stared into his draft. Then: "Wanna smoke?"

"Nah, but I'll go."

The lamps on Front Street cast yellow light on the groups of teenagers that wandered up and down the block, hoping to slip into one of the bars that lined the road. Dave lit a cigarette and nodded to the ones that made eye contact with him as they passed. Nick didn't recognize anyone and looked at his feet. He thought that Dave used to be more careful; a year ago, Dave never would have smoked where the kids could see him.

"What about you, man?" Dave asked after a long drag. "You gonna keep making radio shows that no one listens to for the rest of your life? You still got time to make a nice pension in the military."

"I like my job," Nick said. He pulled down the zipper of his parka and pulled it back up (two, one). He didn't add that he had felt paralyzed by the army's rules and procedures, that the impetus to do everything correctly had completely immobilized him. Dave never really understood that. Instead, he continued, "I think it's important. I like that kids get excited about their stories."

"Yeah, but you got what, like five listeners?"

Nick shrugged. "Where else am I going to get this kind of artistic freedom? They basically let me do whatever I want."

"It's your life, man. There's a lot of opportunity here, but don't overstay. You'll go crazy up here. I been here longer than you."

"Maybe a few more years." Nick shoved his hands in his pockets and looked up at the dark sky. A thin green beam of light shot through the night, forming a tightrope between the street lights.

Dave followed Nick's gaze. The light rippled, sending green waves shimmering across the black sky. "Hey, man," he said, suddenly animated, "that looks like a good one! I bet they're really moving outside of town."

"Wanna go look?" Nick thought the excitement of seeing the northern lights might bring Dave out of his funk. He couldn't tell if Dave was actually leaving Nome or bluffing, but Dave was an outdoorsman, and Nick knew he couldn't resist an excuse to get out of town and onto the land.

"Alright." Dave flicked his cigarette into the snow and ground it out with his heel. "Let's go see what it looks like on the other side of Anvil. Truck's over there." He slapped his coat for his keys; each dull thud cut the air like a drum.

Nick sighed. "I'll drive."

"No, man, I can drive," Dave insisted. "I've only had two."

"I'll drive," Nick said. Dave acquiesced, and two men clamored into the truck, which Dave had left running while they'd been in the bar to prevent the engine from freezing.

Nick adjusted the truck's mirrors (two, one). He took off his hat, smoothed down his hair, and put his hat back on. He tapped each spoke of the steering wheel (four, three, two, one), minutely adjusted the driver's seat, and put on his seatbelt before pulling out of town. The tires crunched through the thin layer of ice on the road as Dave leaned back in the passenger seat and closed his eyes. "You know, man, I just wish there was something more I could do to help. I just don't know what the long-term is going to look like here."

"Caroline's been working at Kawerak for like forty years, right?" Nick asked, referring to Dave's coworker.

"Yeah, but she's like, from here."

"So maybe there should just be more people from here who work there. That way there'll be less turnover, right?"

"I know, I know," Dave grumbled.

"You're always saying inconsistency is the problem." Nick was keeping his eyes on the dark road in front of him to keep his voice calm. "If you leave, those kids'll have one less person to look up to."

"I know, man," Dave said. He sighed. "Maybe I'll come back in a few years."

The two men were approaching the base of Anvil Mountain. "Still going to the other side?" Nick asked.

"Nah, let's just stop at the top. The light pollution doesn't look so bad." Dave sat up straight in his seat to look out the dashboard window. Nick turned on the high beams and began the slow ascent. The road was covered in ice, but still clear. Soon it would be under five or six feet of snow and impossible to drive through.

"I guess I am gonna miss the kids, though," Dave said. "It'll be like leaving behind my sons or something."

"You thinking of starting a family?" Nick asked.

"If I get the right girl. Maybe I'll find one down south."

"She probably won't want to come back here."

"Yeah, well."

"Woah!" Nick slammed on the brakes as a burst of red flashed across the road. "What the hell."

"Those foxes, man. Let's see if it wants to stop for a cig."

"Shut up, man." Nick steered the truck up Anvil Mountain until they hit the plateau. White Alice rose out of the mountain crest a little further ahead, and the four curved towers blocked out the stars and aurora. Nick pulled up next to the base of the massive Cold War remnants and turned off the engine.

"Kill the brights," Dave said. He jumped out of the truck and squinted upward. Nick climbed out of the driver's seat, and the two men stepped over the collapsed fence that circled the White Alice tower campus and crossed to the other side of the mountain, necks craned to keep sight of the northern lights. The fan of green light overhead waved delicately across the night sky, gently skimming the thick black horizon. When Nick first moved to Alaska, he had been shocked to learn that the images he'd seen of the northern lights had been captured by a slow-shutter lens, which caused the entire sky to appear green. In reality, the lights were more like snakes, winding luxuriously over the plane of the sky like slow, satisfied, living things.

"Hey, you know if you whistle at them they're supposed to dance?" Dave asked.

"I did a show on that once, man. It's supposed to be really bad luck. Disrespectful to the land. One guy was cursed for the rest of his life. Someone told me that the lights come down and cut your head off."

"Come on."

Nick shrugged and brushed at his coat. "Hasn't one of your kids said something about it, or knew somebody who whistled at the lights and like, died the next day?"

"Talking foxes, angry lights — it's all bullshit, man. You're going to go back to America and sound like a crazy person."

"Alaska is in America, man. Those stories have stuck around for a reason."

"Whistling is not disrespect. It's more like music, like you're giving them something to dance to."

Nick was silent.

"Jesus, Nick. Your eye is twitching." Dave clapped his hand on Nick's shoulder harder than he intended, jarring Nick forward.

"Just saying," Nick mumbled.

"Saying what? Go on."

"What?" Nick took his gloves off and picked up a hand full of snow. He rubbed the flakes vigorously between his hands (one two three one two three). The rhythm let him think. The worst thing that could happen to him at this moment was Dave would decide to leave Nome, and if he whistled, he would be punished with the worst thing. But if he didn't whistle, Dave might lose respect for him and head south anyway (one two three one two three).

"Well, I sure as hell can't whistle, but I know you can." Dave crossed his arms. Overhead, white light intermingled with the green, forming languid patterns in the sky.

"Come on, man, let's go back."

Dave sat down in the snow. Nick's scarf had frozen to his mouth. He was sweating in the cold. Okay, he thought. It's just a whistle. He could whistle and still be a good person, a person who was dedicating his career to honoring the land and the people who lived on it. Maybe that was enough.

"Alright, man," Nick said. "Get up. I'll whistle and we'll go."

"Make 'em dance!"

"You know nothing's going to happen, right?"

"I know, man. It'll be good for you. Give you a little bit of your sanity back."

Nick pulled his scarf down and gasped as the cold bit at his lips. He glanced at Dave, then put two fingers in his mouth and whistled. The clear arc of sound swept over the land toward the slithering lights, echoed off the peaks of the range, and ricocheted off the ice. Silence enveloped the two men on the mountain as the whistle journeyed upward into the night. Their eyes followed it skyward. The translucent, liquid green and white lights continued to fan over the dark sphere of the sky. "See?" Dave said triumphantly. He stood. "Fucking freezing out here. Let's go back." Nick continued to gaze in the direction of his whistle, absently pulling at the zipper of his coat (two, one; two, one).

Dave managed to take a few steps toward the White Alice towers before the lights began to change. The green lights brightened and swallowed up the white lights, forming thick emerald ribbons of light that sliced through the dome of the sky. "Hey," Nick said quietly, and Dave stopped and looked up in time to see the roiling aurora begin to shudder and squirm. The vivid snakes of light arched and convulsed over the tundra as they tore across the sky toward Nome. A neon flash burst over Nick's head, illuminating the mountains, roads, town, and sea.

Dave's terrified face showed in stark relief. Behind him, the White Alice towers flashed bright green.

Then, suddenly, the lights cut out. Nick and Dave were left in blinding darkness.

"Holy shit," Dave whispered.

Nick cleared his throat and knelt on the ice. His hands were numb, but he took another handful of snow and washed them thoroughly (three two one three two one). He didn't feel the snow crystals as they scraped his bare fingers. The darkness lifted, and the men faced the starlit night under the watchful eye of Ursa Major.

"Let's go back," Dave said quietly. "I'll drive." He led the way back over the broken fence and through the White Alice campus. "What the fuck was that? Shit's crazy, man. I can't wait to get out of this place."

Nick shook his head. The men climbed into the truck, and Nick rested his head against the side window as Dave began to navigate down the mountain. He saw a flash of green out of the corner of his eye and turned to see a snake of light streak south over the Bering Sea, disappearing below the horizon. He knew now, without a doubt, that Dave would soon follow it down to the Lower 48 at his first opportunity.

"Hey, let's go get another beer," Nick said hopefully.

"Nah, I'm gonna turn in," Dave answered, keeping his eyes on the road. Nick nodded and looked out the window again, searching for any last remnant of the northern lights, but all he saw across the sea was darkness.

■ ■ ■

anvil tavern

EILEEN'S FAVORITE GAME WAS TO SEE how much gold she could collect in a single night. She looked forward to the early morning hours when the crowd spilled out of Breakers and into Anvil Tavern, her family's new restaurant and bar, to eat her sister's increasingly famous kimchi wings and short ribs for their after-midnight price. Eileen took drink orders while the miners and their girls jostled each other to look at the menu and shout over the amateur DJ. And, inevitably, one or two men would come in with a freshly cleaned vial of gold flakes to show off and end up shaking a portion of their cleanup into Eileen's hand as they leaned over the bar to tell her that she was the prettiest girl they'd ever seen. She would smile, put the gold in her pocket, and add it to her collection after she climbed the stairs to her bedroom on the second floor of the restaurant at the end of the night.

Anvil Tavern had been open for three months when Eileen's sister, Maggie, found Eileen's gold collection while she was snooping around her room looking for a hairbrush. She confronted Eileen as she prepped the bar downstairs. "Leenie," Maggie said, holding up a Campbell's Soup can with almost an inch of gold at the bottom, "this is a fortune. You have to sell this."

"It's not that much," Eileen shrugged. "I think I'm going to have someone turn it into a necklace or something."

"Seriously, Leenie. Just go see how much this is worth."

※ ※ ※

Eileen took her gold collection to the trader a few weeks later. The door was locked, but just as she was about to turn away, the trader shoved up the service window. Early fall rain clung to his grizzled red beard, mingling with his sweat. "Yeah?"

Eileen took a deep breath. "I would like to sell."

"Sell what, honey?" the man asked, looking at her chest.

"My gold." Eileen held out her can. The man's yellow eyes flicked up to her face.

"Even better," he said. "Come on in." The door unlocked automatically and Eileen pushed it open.

Inside, the man held out his enormous leathery hand and shook Eileen's small pale one. "Pleased to meet you. Name's Keith."

"Eileen."

"Eileen, huh? Well, Eileen, this way." He led her through the front of the shop and into a wood-paneled back room. The brown floor was tracked with huge muddy footprints. A single brown table with a small scale on it stood in the center of the room, surrounded by three chairs. Keith pulled out one of the chairs for Eileen, and she sat obediently. The trader circled the table to sit on the other side. "Can I see that can?"

Eileen handed it over.

"How'd you get so much gold?"

"People give it to me as tips at the bar."

"Oh yeah, I guess I have seen you around. You're at Anvil Tavern? Breakers sometimes?" Eileen nodded. "You chose a real good time to sell," Keith said. "The market price is pretty high." He shook the can and held it to his nose. "It looks like it's all clean, no extra dirt. We take ten percent — you know that?"

"No."

"Sorry, honey, you're not gonna get a better rate anywhere else."

"Okay." Eileen looked down and shifted in her chair. She didn't want to spend much more time with this huge man by herself. Only Maggie knew where she was.

The door in the front of the shop slammed open. "Anybody in here?" A tall, broad blond man swaggered into the back room. He raised his eyebrows when he saw Eileen. "Sorry, Keith, didn't realize you had company."

"She's sellin' gold, Jim," Keith said.

"Selling gold? How'd you get that gold, little lady?"

"Tips at the bar," Keith answered. "It's rightly hers."

The blond miner held his hands up. "Never said it wasn't. I got some stuff to sell, too. And I want to enter the lottery."

"Lottery?" Eileen sat up straighter. Her parents sold scratch-off tickets for a dollar after hours at their restaurant, but she didn't know that there was an official lottery in town. Maybe they could sell lottery tickets too.

"Never you mind," Keith growled. Eileen shifted nervously in her seat, feeling like she was caught in the middle of a prior argument between the two men.

"Nah, Keith, don't play her like that," Jim said loudly. "Show her the nugget."

Keith scuffed his shoe on the brown floor, leaving a dark skid mark.

"Fine. I'll tell her, you dirty crook." Jim turned to Eileen, his blue eyes crinkling around the edges. "Keith here runs a little lottery at the end of the summer mining season. That's actually coming up here pretty soon. If you sell gold here, you can enter your name on a ticket. My nephew draws the winner right before the ice comes in. If you win, you get the biggest nugget of the season. Old Keith here's always got a few favorites, so he don't tell that many people about it." He grinned. "Keith, show her the nugget."

Keith glared at Jim but couldn't resist showing off his treasure. He reached into the breast pocket of his coat, fumbled around for a moment, then drew out the largest hunk of gold Eileen had ever seen. It sat heavily in the palm of his hand. "This is the same one we used last year," Keith said. "The winners sold it right back to us and nothin' this season compares."

Eileen nodded, trying not to look too impressed. "How do I enter?"

"Let me count your gold first, then you can fill out a ticket." Keith dumped the contents of the can out onto the scale. "Mmm-hmmm," he said. "That's over two thousand dollars you've got here."

"Lemme see," Jim circled around the back of the register. "Yeah, shit." He clapped Keith on the back.

"So I get eighteen hundred?" Eileen asked.

Jim rolled his eyes at the ceiling. "Jesus, Keith, I fuckin' knew it. Rate's actually eight percent, sweetheart."

Keith glared up at Jim. "I must've forgot," he said slowly. "Our rate is eight percent." He stood up and disappeared into the front of the shop.

"Sometimes you gotta watch out for old Keith," Jim said to Eileen as he took the trader's seat. "So this is all from tips?"

"Yes, I work behind the bar at Anvil Tavern. And I fill in at Breakers too sometimes if they need somebody."

"You're one of the Nowikis?"

"Yes, Phil Nowiki is my father." She was surprised that he knew anything about her family.

"Gee, so first you guys own a couple'a restaurants and now you're expanding into selling gold too? Leave something for the rest of us." Jim winked at Eileen, and Eileen smiled back nervously. "Seriously, though," he continued, "you guys must be making a killing."

"No," Eileen said. "It costs a lot to keep our bars so clean and new. And shipping food and alcohol up here is very expensive, you know, because we can only barge or fly it. And we have to pay our workers. We're not rich. And there is competition. We don't own the town."

"Well, you've got quite the gig. Owning two of the nicest bars here ain't nothin'."

"We work a lot."

"So do a lot of people. But you gotta have some fun, too. All kinds of neat things to do up here you can't do anywhere else."

"I have fun." Eileen looked at her lap. "I talk to my sister."

"You take good care of us."

"Alright." Jim stood up, and Keith lumbered back around the table to take his seat back. The trader produced a wad of bills from his pocket and shuffled them. "One thousand, eight hundred and fifty-four dollars, forty-six cents," he pronounced, leaving the cash in front of Eileen. Eileen quickly folded it into the front pocket of her jeans.

"And the ticket?" Jim prompted.

"And the ticket," Keith said. He handed Eileen a small blue carnival ticket. "Put your name and phone number on it. We'll call you if you win."

Eileen quickly scribbled her name and phone number on the blue piece of paper. "Thank you," she said, more to Jim than to Keith.

"Pleasure," Jim said.

Eileen stood, shook Keith's hand, smiled at Jim, and left the shop. She put her cash in a book in her room.

That night Eileen started her shift at the bar early. The restaurant had been empty for most of the day, but she knew they would have more customers once the Permanent Fund Dividend checks were distributed in the fall and people from the surrounding villages came to Nome to visit relatives and pick up supplies. Usually the PFD season was marked by stress and overcrowding in her family's bar, but she was actually excited for the checks to come out this year: it was a chance to show off Anvil Tavern to people from all over Western Alaska. Eileen and Maggie had designed the bar based on pictures of bars and restaurants in New York City they had found online, and Eileen was proud of their work. The bar had modern, textured walls, low industrial lights, and mirrors strategically placed to make the main room appear bigger than it was. It transitioned well from being a restaurant in the daytime to a bar at night due to the two enormous windows that flanked the bar on either side — one faced Front Street, and one opened up onto the Bering Sea — so patrons could watch night fall. In the summer months, the girls pulled down the shades on the windows in the evening to create the illusion of darkness outside.

The family business had been divided in two since Anvil Tavern opened. Her father kept the books for both, but her mother had her own staff at the family's original restaurant and didn't need Eileen or Maggie to help there anymore. She rarely came to Anvil Tavern, so Eileen and Maggie managed the place on their own. The sisters strove to differentiate their bar and restaurant from their mother's establishment by appealing to a younger crowd. Eileen had named the bar Anvil Tavern after Anvil Rock, the flat-topped rock formation that balanced on the peak of Anvil Mountain just outside of Nome. Anvil Rock stood sentry above the town, integral to the town's identity and sense of place but above it and apart from it. Eileen wanted Anvil Tavern to emulate its namesake, to be part of the community but above the everyday. The restaurant wasn't paying for itself yet, but the bar was full every night.

"Eileen," Maggie called from the back. "What're you thinking about over there?"

"Nothing, just cleaning up."

"You okay?"

"Yep."

Maggie came out from the kitchen, wiping her hands on her chef's pants. "Did something happen today?"

Eileen coughed. "I sold my gold," she admitted.

"What? How much did you make?"

"A little bit," Eileen said. She didn't know how she wanted to spend the money yet, so didn't want to give away too much.

"That's great! Should we buy those tablecloths we saw online? Or would those look too cheap? Wait, no, you should buy something for yourself first. Maybe one of those Eskimo love bracelets? I've seen you looking at them at Maruskiya's." Maggie paused, then giggled. "Or you could get this guy to buy one for you." She jerked her chin up past Eileen's shoulder. "Make sure he pays you in cash." Eileen blushed but waited to turn around to see who Maggie was talking about. She was glad they had been speaking in Tagalog, so that the customer wouldn't understand.

Maggie disappeared into the kitchen, and Eileen turned to face the bar. She coughed when she saw Jim leaning over the edge of the counter. "Hi there," he said, his voice quieter than it had been in the gold shop. "Just thought I'd come by. I'll have an Alaskan White, please."

"Okay." Eileen grabbed a bottle from the fridge, popped the top off, and handed it to him.

"That's a pretty shirt. Don't see too many girls wearing shirts like that around here," Jim said, leaving his beer on the counter.

"Thanks," Eileen said. "I order them from the Philippines."

"Do you miss it?" he asked. "I mean, do you like being here?"

"I was actually born in Spokane, and I've never been to the Philippines. We came up to Nome when I was two or three, I think. I like it, but I think I'd like to live in California someday, or maybe go to Seattle for college."

"You went to school here? High school? You know, you look Native to me. You could probably just say you were Native."

Eileen shrugged. "My mom's Filipino," she said, "and my dad's Polish. And yes," she continued, answering Jim's first question. "I mean I've lived here my whole life. I went through Anvil City Science Academy and the high school. I graduated two years ago, and we just opened this bar at the beginning of the summer. We used to cook for all the events at school, like basketball games and fund-raisers. Kind of like free advertising for our first restaurant. We did so well that we got to open this one. I designed it."

"*Bunso*! So chatty out there!" Maggie called from the kitchen in Tagalog. Eileen looked away from Jim, embarrassed. She expected him to drink his Alaskan White and leave.

Instead, he pushed his beer away from him. "Do you have a four wheeler?" he asked.

"No, I don't think we would use it. I mean, I've ridden on one before."

"Look," Jim said, leaning so far over the bar that he was nearly standing, "I'd like to take you out sometime. Wanna go for a ride tomorrow afternoon? If you're not working?" He sat back and took a swig of beer, studiously avoiding eye contact with Eileen.

"Oh." Eileen looked down. "Well, it's almost PFD season, and we've got a lot of cleaning to do."

Maggie appeared at Eileen's elbow. "Of course she'll go," Maggie said. "She'd love to. Right, Leenie?"

Eileen turned to Jim and smiled. "I'd love to," she said.

■ ■ ■

WHEN JIM PULLED UP IN FRONT OF ANVIL TAVERN THE NEXT afternoon, Eileen was waiting outside in her rain jacket. It was chilly even for early fall, and the day was overcast.

"Hey there," Jim greeted her, killing the engine. "I thought you might wear some cute little thing, so I brought you some real clothes." He hopped off the ATV and pulled an oversized Carhartt jacket and gloves from the storage unit in the back. "Put these on."

"Hi," Eileen said, accepting the clothes instinctively. "I don't think I need these," she said. "I'll be okay."

"No, you won't. Oh, and you have to wear this." Jim tossed her a red helmet.

"Really?" Eileen laughed. She had never worn a helmet while riding a four wheeler before.

"Really." Jim took the helmet from Eileen's hands and placed it squarely on her head. His calloused fingers grazed her chin as he fiddled with the straps, and Eileen blushed as he examined the fit of the helmet. "Should do it. Want to protect that pretty little head of yours." He winked as Eileen's blush deepened. "Get on there."

Eileen climbed onto the back of the ATV, and Jim slid on in front of her. "Hold on to me, now," he called. She circled her arms around his waist. He was lean and wiry from summers fighting the Bering Sea for gold, and as he turned the vehicle on, she grasped his torso tightly.

Jim pulled slowly out of town but kicked into full gear once they reached the Nome-Teller Road. Eileen rested the bill of her helmet against his back to keep the wind out of her face so she could breathe. Jim's knuckles were a bloodless white marked with red spots, and Eileen wondered how he was driving the four wheeler without gloves. "Where are we going?" she shouted in Jim's ear.

"The windmills!" he yelled back. He turned sharply off the road and jogged the vehicle down the highway shoulder. Eileen loosened her grip so she could absorb the shocks of the ride. The reds, golds, and browns of the autumn tundra streaked by them as Jim maneuvered toward Anvil Mountain. Eileen used the reindeer moss that sprung up from the tundra to keep time, each white patch representing one foot further from her home. The air was heavy with rain, and droplets formed on the ATV and on Eileen's helmet. She shivered in her too-large coat.

Suddenly Jim pulled up short. Eileen lifted the brim of her helmet off his back to see why they had stopped. "What's wrong?" she asked.

"See those guys over there? That's the way we gotta go," Jim said, pointing to three figures and a vehicle further up the tundra path. "Just tryn'a figure out who they are." He paused, then inched cautiously forward until Eileen could make out two men and a woman, barely visible against the mottled tundra, standing beside a small stream. Each of the three held a black plastic gold pan full of rocks. Eileen was sure she'd never seen any of them in either of her family's bars before.

"Jim!" one of the men shouted as they approached. "Thought that was you!"

"Rocky," Jim nodded to the man. "This is Eileen."

"Nice to meet you." The woman grinned at Eileen, revealing several missing teeth in her lined red face.

"Nice to meet you, too," Eileen responded, smiling back politely. She felt her heart beat anxiously in her chest but was able to keep her breath steady.

"Gettin' anything good?" Jim asked.

"Just dirt so far, but this creek looks pretty promising," Rocky said, leering at Eileen. Eileen lowered the brim of her helmet to shield herself against his hollow green-and-yellow stare.

"Well, we'll leave you to it. Just goin' up to check on those windmills," Jim said. He kicked the ATV back to life. Once they had bumped along for a safe distance, Jim looked back at Eileen over his shoulder and said, "Meth heads." Eileen nodded weakly.

They were climbing the mountain steadily now, pushing against the occasional gust that cascaded southward down the mountain. The Bering Sea and southern portions of Nome were lost in the fog behind them. Eileen peeked over Jim's shoulder and saw the windmill farm ahead. The tall, steel frames were just a shade darker than the sky and threw no shadows in the thin light. Behind them, she could make out the tips of the White Alice towers gleaming with condensation.

"Ever been up here?" Jim called over his shoulder.

"No!" the wind carried Eileen's words back toward the invisible town. She put the bill of her helmet back against Jim's shoulders to shield her face against the wind.

When Eileen lifted her head again, they had reached the plateau. The windmills, which had looked small and distant from Front Street, were enormous, their wide metal beams planted yards apart on the permafrost. Jim drove to the center of the industrial forest and killed the engine. The windmill blades were still despite the gale. Jim jumped off the four wheeler and turned to help Eileen climb off the back seat. He held her elbow for a moment too long once she was steady on her feet, so that she turned to look at him. He quickly kissed her cheek. They both immediately blushed and smiled mirrored self-conscious smiles. Eileen held her breath. He reached under her chin to undo the helmet. She pulled the helmet off and left it on the front seat of the ATV.

Jim had to fight against the wind to make his way over to the nearest windmill tower. "Check this out!" he shouted as he grabbed the thin metal ladder that ran up the tower to just beneath the windmill blades. "I climbed all the way to the top of this one once."

"That's so high!" Eileen said, looking up. Even as she watched, the blades of the windmill became obscured by rising fog. She didn't think she would be able to climb that high; she would have too much difficulty breathing as she neared the top.

"Well, I helped build 'em," Jim said. "That's the reason I got up here to Nome, actually, was to help with these things. Shame they don't really work like they're supposed to."

"What do you mean? Aren't they generating wind power?"

"Not enough to make them viable, unfortunately. Kinda depressing. But lemme show you something." Jim grabbed Eileen's hand and pulled her to the other side of the mountain. Eileen followed gamely but had to concentrate on putting one foot in front of the other; she felt the wind would blow her off the plateau at any moment if she lost focus.

They stopped abruptly a few feet from the edge of a sheer drop-off. Whereas the foothills surrounding the windmill plateau were soft and rolling, this ledge looked too steep to hike down. Eileen stood on her toes to look over the edge of the cliff. The tundra appeared smooth and washed out on the ground below, but there were no distinguishing features on the land to give her any hint of how high the cliff actually might be.

Jim let go of Eileen's hand. She gave him a small, apprehensive smile. "Okay!" he said, spreading his arms to reveal his full wingspan. "So this takes a little bit of faith, but just watch me." Eileen stiffened as he moved toward her, but just as he seemed about to embrace her, he pivoted and raced toward the edge of the cliff. Eileen shrieked as Jim bent his knees and launched himself off the ledge and toward the murky ground below. He hung in the air for a moment, then turned and waved at Eileen before dropping out of sight. Eileen stood rooted to the mountain. She was having trouble breathing. Jim had seemed perfectly happy the whole drive up to the windmills; what would make him want to jump off the edge of a cliff? Should she take his ATV to the police station? Would she even be able to drive the four wheeler over the tundra? Before Eileen could recover her breath, however, Jim reappeared in the sky right in front of the cliff. The wind propelled him forward until he landed lightly on both feet. He stumbled a few steps away from the ledge, then dropped his arms and grinned triumphantly at Eileen.

Eileen stared at him. "You're crazy," she said. "How is that even possible?"

"Buddy of mine almost fell from this spot once. The wind saved him. I don't know much about physics, but I do know that this works. It's great. Wanna try?"

"I don't think so," Eileen said. She took a small step backward. Now that she knew Jim was still alive, her chest felt even tighter, and she began to gasp as if the air was being compressed out of her lungs. She breathed as quietly as she could so that Jim wouldn't notice and prayed that the gasping would not turn into a full asthma attack.

"Come on, I'll be right behind you. I have killer reflexes. Here, let me show you again." Jim threw out his arms and bounded off the ledge. This time, the wind caught his chest just inches away from the cliff face and threw him back to solid ground immediately. "Simple as that," Jim said. "Your turn. I'll be right here, don't you worry."

"But I didn't see how it worked," Eileen protested. "What if it only works for you because you're bigger than me? You have more surface area?"

"Well, like I said, I'll catch you. Don't you worry. I'll be right here." Jim smiled reassuringly.

A rush of oxygen flooded Eileen's brain as she regained her normal breathing rhythm. Suddenly she was wide awake and full of energy. "Okay," she said. Maybe if he saw her doing something daring, he would forget about her weak lungs. "Okay." She spread her arms, took two steps forward, and poked the toes of her rain boots over the ledge. She didn't look down. Instead, she focused on a white line of snow that cut through the brown tundra on the mountain range ahead of her. As the next gust of wind hit her back, Eileen closed her eyes and leaned forward.

Her heels caught the rock cliff before she swung into open air. For a horrible moment her mind went blank, and she lost her breath and fell freely toward the tundra below. She felt her hair stream out behind her and thought, I am going to die. Then she belly-flopped into an elastic wall of wind. The force of the invisible barrier repelled her upward, and she lurched back onto the cliff, dazed and soaked from the fog. Jim caught her before she fell backwards, his rough hands almost entirely encircling her arms. "That was a good one!" he said.

Eileen felt like she was choking. There was so much wind that she couldn't quite claim any air for herself. She looked up at Jim and inhaled shallowly, then doubled over and heaved. Once she could breathe again, she flushed a deep red and stood up hurriedly. Jim took a few steps toward her, looking concerned.

"I want to go home," she said.

⁂

Jim showed up at Anvil Tavern every night for a week after their failed date, and every night Eileen gave him only the necessary amount of attention. He sat dejectedly at the corner of the bar, hoping she would speak to him, until one of his friends would show up and lure him away to play pool or sit at one of the tables in the back. Every night he left Eileen a tip in gold, and every night she would wait for him to leave before putting his gold flakes in her pocket.

On the seventh day, Jim didn't show up at Anvil Tavern at his normal six o'clock time. Eileen was disappointed, but Maggie encouraged her: "Good, looks like he got the message. If he weren't so good-looking, he would've been kinda creepy, Leenie. Well, plenty of fish in the sea." Eileen nodded and continued to store her gold tips in the can in her room.

⁂

A few weeks later, when the sun was rising mid-morning and the autumn air had yielded to the arctic winter, Eileen opened Anvil Tavern at noon. A tall, weathered miner wandered in just as Eileen was writing the daily specials on the board above the bar. Eileen recognized Keith and greeted him warmly. "I have some more gold to sell," she said as she handed him his Alaskan Stout and set a glass on the bar counter. "I can put in another entry for the lottery."

"No need, sweetheart," Keith said. He looked around the empty restaurant. "Season's over. The nugget's yours." He took a swig of beer straight from the bottle. "Jim's little nephew pulled your name out of the hat. Shows you some people have all the luck."

He pulled the hunk of gold out of his coat pocket and set it down on the bar. Eileen stared at it. "Are you sure?"

Keith drained half his beer. "Eileen Nowiki, right? Ain't no other Eileen Nowikis in this town." Eileen thought with surprise that he seemed almost tender toward her. Kind of proud, even. He held his beer bottle up to cover his face. "Well, missy," he said, smacking his tongue against his teeth, "you can come right back to me and sell it if you want. I'll just be in the shop."

"Um, okay," Eileen said. "Thank you."

"Doesn't make a lick of difference to me." Keith set his empty bottle on the bar. "Good luck to you." He left without paying. Eileen stared after him, wide-eyed.

"Eileen! Can you look at this for a minute? Do you think these'll sell?" Maggie barged into the bar from the kitchen, waving a small plate of fried potato skins. Her eyes flashed to the hunk of gold sitting on the bar, and she stopped short. "Sweet Jesus," she breathed. "What is that?"

"I won the lottery," Eileen said dumbly.

"What do you mean?"

"When I sold my gold, they put my name in a lottery to win this," she gestured to the nugget. "It's a lottery they have every year."

Maggie picked up the nugget and held it close to her face. "It's so heavy," she said finally.

"I know."

"How much do you think it's worth?"

"I'm not sure. This is probably, what, seven times as much as my gold flakes were? I can't tell."

Maggie shook her head, still holding the nugget up to her eye. "You have to tell Mom and Dad. But seriously, buy yourself something first before they make you spend it all on the restaurants."

"I'll tell them," Eileen said. "And I don't want to sell it for a little while anyway. Gold prices are pretty low right now." She did not admit that she had found herself listening eagerly to the thrice-daily gold reports on KNOM for the past week, so she could choose the best time to sell the small flakes stashed in her room.

Maggie handed the nugget to her. Eileen felt its surprising weight press against her palm. "Well, at least get it out of here. Bring it to your room, and I'll mind the bar while you hide it."

"Thanks!" Eileen dashed upstairs and put the nugget in her can, where it roosted on top of her other gold pieces like a mother hen.

Jim came into Anvil Tavern that night with a group of miners Eileen half-recognized. He ordered an Alaskan

White and slid forward eagerly on his stool. "Congratulations, Eileen!" he shouted down the bar. "No one deserves it more than you!"

Eileen popped his beer open and handed it to him. "On what?" she asked cagily.

"The nugget, baby! You won the nugget!"

Eileen started, then blushed. "How did you know?"

"My nephew pulls the winning name, remember? Plus, everyone knows. This was a big day for us here miners." Jim slapped the bar jovially, then leaned forward and motioned for Eileen to come over. "Look," he said in a low voice, "some people aren't happy about it. You're not a miner, and you only cashed gold once. Nothing for you to worry about," he added, seeing Eileen's alarmed expression. "Just thought you should know."

"Jim!" one of his friends shouted from the pool tables.

"Gotta go, sweetheart." Jim winked at Eileen and slid off the stool before Eileen could find her voice to respond.

■ ■ ■

THE NEXT MORNING, MAGGIE BURST INTO EILEEN'S ROOM. "Leenie! Leenie!" she yelled, shaking her younger sister's shoulder.

"What?" It was dark outside, and Eileen had stayed up late to clean the bar.

"Leenie, come with me. Someone broke the front window."

Eileen sat straight up in bed and gathered her blanket around her. She followed Maggie down the stairs to the bar and was shocked awake by a blast of cold air. Maggie had turned on all the lights, and Eileen felt her breath catch when she saw the damage. The window that looked out on Front Street lay on the restaurant floor in a jagged waste. Snow streamed through the broken window and swirled among the shards of glass. Skid lines on the floor led to a stray brick in the far corner. Eileen let out her breath and tried to draw another but couldn't. She sat down and put her head between her knees, and Maggie squatted to put an arm around her. The sisters pressed their heads together. "What're we going to tell Mom and Dad?"

Eileen squeezed her eyes tight so that she could concentrate on breathing. "I don't know," she managed. "I can sell the nugget to repair the window —" Eileen's eyes widened. "The nugget!" She pressed her forehead into her knees.

"What?" Maggie asked. "What about the nugget?"

"I didn't deserve the nugget!" Eileen gasped into her thighs. "They thought Jim rigged the contest so that I would get the nugget."

"Did he?" Maggie asked.

"I don't know!" Eileen said. She calmed herself down by forming a plan. "We can use some of the money from the nugget to repair the window, but it's not really that much money. No one's ever going to want to come to Anvil Tavern ever again." Her breath came back but in quick, sputtering lurches. "We'll lose it!" She dug her face into Maggie's shoulder, and Maggie stroked her hair.

"Well," Maggie said carefully, "nothing to do but clean it up. Let's get this window covered before any more snow gets in." She waited until Eileen could draw a few long, shaky breaths, then held her hands out to help her up. "And then we'll call Myra and take those assholes to court."

Eileen sighed. "It'll be too late for the restaurant anyway."

Eileen and Maggie were still evaluating the window when a police car drove up to the snowy curb on Front Street. One of the officers who patrolled the bars nightly got out of the car and stared grimly at the mess from outside the restaurant. "Maggie, Eileen," he said through the broken window. "What's going on here?"

"Someone broke the window!" Maggie called to him in English.

"Mm-hmm. Any idea who did it?"

"Gold miners," Maggie said.

"Maggie!" Eileen admonished.

"Come on. We have to tell them." Maggie turned back to the policeman. "Eileen here won the gold nugget, and now people are mad at us."

The officer nodded. "The lottery. I thought it was next week. Well, we'll have someone check in on you two throughout the day to make sure you're both safe. Do you want someone to stay outside the restaurant here now?"

"No thanks," Maggie said. "Sun's almost up."

"Alright. When you're done here, come on down to the station and file a report."

"We will."

The policeman nodded again and retreated to the warmth of his vehicle.

Eileen and Maggie went back upstairs to put on parkas and snow pants over their pajamas. "He should have offered to help," Maggie grumbled. "God, I need some coffee."

※ ※ ※

THE SUN HAD RISEN OVER THE BERING SEA TO GLARE OVER Nome with a flat, white light by the time the sisters had swept the floor of the bar and hung a tarp over the window. Reporters from KNOM and the *Nome Nugget* had knocked on the restaurant door, and Eileen had given them both candid interviews. The first interview would play on the radio with the afternoon news. Neither of the sisters wanted to listen to it.

Their parents had come before dawn to ensure that Eileen had a plan for repairing the damage and had been both relieved and angry she had won the nugget. Her father had surveyed the inside of Anvil Tavern with his hands on his hips. "Well, this one wasn't doing so well anyway," her father had said. "Those windows were too expensive. We weren't going to be able to insulate them well enough once it got really cold. This room would have been bleeding heat. You knew that, Eileen. The insurance deductible is going to set this place back, and I'm not sure we're going to be able to heat it at all. Maybe we'll just shut it down now and reopen in May."

Eileen took shallower and shallower breaths as the day progressed. Closing from December to May would ruin the new business. Maggie called their staff to tell them they wouldn't be getting any shifts until the spring. The Nowikis would have to work quickly to repair the restaurant if they ever hoped to open it again at all; winter was fast approaching, and they needed the window to protect the building interior. Eileen knew she had to sell the nugget to make the repairs, but she didn't think she could face Keith again in the traders' shop.

⬛ ⬛ ⬛

EILEEN STOOD DEJECTEDLY BEHIND THE BAR THAT EVENING, watching the tarp over the window flutter against the sea breeze. A tap on her shoulder made her jump. "Hey boss," one of the kitchen staff, Morris, said cheerfully. He must have come through the back door. Two of Anvil Tavern's regular cooks peered eagerly over his shoulder. "Can we get started?"

"Huh?" Eileen asked. She looked at her watch, and was surprised to see it was half an hour before the restaurant usually opened for dinner. "Didn't Maggie call you?"

The back door swung open, and one of their weekday waitresses rushed in. "Hey guys," she said. "Sorry I'm late!"

"Yeah, she did," Morris said, "but then we heard on KNOM that we were open. You could've given us a head's up. Thought about not coming to work today, but after all that talk, I thought I'd better."

"What? Did they play the interview?"

"There were a couple of things about it. One guy came on and said he was really sorry, but you'd won that gold lottery thing fair and square, and you needed some help getting the restaurant back together. Then they played your interview all tearful and it broke this old man's heart. You didn't listen?"

Eileen shook her head. She couldn't speak.

"Well, I bet we get a few people in tonight at least." The three men and the waitress filed into the kitchen.

"Hey, Maggie!" Eileen called upstairs. "Can you c'mere for a second?"

Maggie appeared in the stairwell, eyes heavy with sleep. "What's up?"

"Your crew's here. They're in the kitchen preparing appetizers."

"What the hell?" Maggie asked. "I don't think we can pay them." She hurried down to the kitchen.

Eileen was about to follow when she heard a knock at the front door of the bar. She sighed when she saw Jim grinning at her through the small door window and shook her head at him. "Eileen!" he shouted. "Might want to open a little early today!"

"What?" she yelled back.

"Open early!" He waved through the glass. Annoyed, she crossed the restaurant to open the door. He hopped inside and made a move like he was going to give her a hug. Instead, he stretched his arm away from her, down Front Street. "Look," he said.

Eileen peered around his shoulder and gasped. Over a hundred people were quietly lined up outside the restaurant. "You open?" an older woman yelled. "We're starving!"

Eileen quickly bowed back behind Jim. "What did you do?" she asked.

"They wanted to help," Jim said, his grin widening.

Eileen nodded brusquely and ducked around him to face the line. "We're open!" she yelled, and to her amazement, the crowd actually cheered.

The restaurant was fully seated within ten minutes, and Eileen had collected reservations through the end of the night. Many customers shoved packages of frozen meat, greens, and casserole into Eileen's hands before she seated them, which made her blush in confusion. The restaurant was freezing, and most customers left their parkas and gloves on as they ate, but everyone smiled and laughed as if enjoying a normal meal. Eileen's mother had come over as soon as she had caught sight of the line. "Wow," she said to Eileen before bustling off to take a party's order. "I didn't think people here liked us this much."

Jim sat at the bar sipping a single Alaskan White while Eileen escorted people to their seats and took drink orders. "Thank you for going on KNOM today," Eileen said when the second round of customers were seated. "You didn't have to."

"No problem," Jim shrugged. "I felt bad." The waitress passed the bar and handed Eileen a list of drink orders on her way to the kitchen. Jim put both his hands on the bar and stood. "Do you think maybe you'd like to go out with me again? Give me another chance?" He winked at her, but Eileen could see that his eyes were earnest.

Eileen surveyed the bustling restaurant. She was exhausted, and couldn't think of what she wanted. It was taking all her energy just to stay on her feet and process the drink orders. She liked that Jim was staring at her expectantly, waiting for her decision. "Hmm," she said vaguely. "If the restaurant closes, then I'm going to take my lottery money and go down to Seattle. If the restaurant stays open, I might stay here with you. I guess we'll have to see."

"Well, I know you're proud of this place and you love your sister and your family, and I know that I want to get to know you better," Jim said, leaning over the counter. "And I also know I screwed up, and that you've been thinking about going to Seattle since way before I started hanging around. But let me try to get you to stay, okay?"

Eileen blushed and looked down. "Okay."

"Okay." Jim took a deep breath. "Hand me that towel back there, would ya? Time to start clearing off these tables so all these folks can get some dinner."

❖ ❖ ❖

the ones who stay

"WAIT WAIT WAIT, I'M GOING WITH you," Christina interrupted, swinging her legs off the arm of the couch. Lynn and Suze looked over at her from the kitchen table, annoyed. "What? I'm going with you," she said. "I don't know this guy, and I've lived here my whole life. You are not about to go hiking way out of town with a strange man." She frowned pointedly at Suze. "I mean, seriously, you don't see the issue with this? You said he's been here for years, and I've never met him? There might be a reason. I'm coming too."

Suze turned to Lynn for support but found Lynn nodding along with Christina. "Fine, fine," Suze said. She shook her hair and pulled it into a bun.

"Is he white or Native?"

"White."

"Hmm. I definitely don't know this guy."

Suze sighed. "Wanna try one of these?" she asked. She held up one of the pieces of fry bread she and Lynn had made.

"For sure." Christina hopped off the couch and joined the other two women at the table. Lynn got up to stir the caribou chili cooking on the stovetop. "How did you learn how to make this?" Christina asked, examining her piece of golden dough. "It looks like a doughnut."

"My mom taught me. We always eat fry bread with chili. The caribou just makes it, like, more Alaskan," Lynn said. She dipped a spoon into the chili and held it up to her nose. "I think this is ready, if you guys don't mind it being like really hot."

"You know what would make this more Alaskan," Christina said, "is Pilot Bread."

Lynn shuddered. "It's so dry!"

"Girl, if you're going to live here you've gotta get used to it."

"Thanks for letting us use your kitchen," Suze said. "The new rotational nurses are kind of unfriendly."

"Yeah, no problem. My roommates went to camp, so I'm all by myself." Christina dunked her fry bread in the chili and put it right in her mouth. "Hot! Hot! But woah, this is good! And healthy too, right? Just caribou and beans?"

"And a whole can of bacon grease," Suze smirked.

Lynn cupped her hand around her mouth and whispered dramatically, "I've been saving it for weeks in our fridge."

"Maybe that's why the new nurses hate you guys. Wow that's so disgusting. But also so delicious." Christina turned to Suze. "So, where are we going?"

Suze shrugged. "Well, Nick —"

"Radio Station Nick, right? DJ in the afternoon?" Christina asked. "Sorry, I'm starting to lose track."

Suze frowned. "Shut up," she said. "And yeah. Don't you listen to KNOM?"

"Uh, no."

"Whatever. Radio Station Nick said he saw this cave when he was flying in a helicopter with some kind of agriculturalist who counts muskoxen or something for one of his radio shows this week, and he wanted to see if he could go find it and climb into it. Doesn't it sound like he has such a cool job?"

"And where did you meet this Radio Station Nick?"

"Um, he's Courtney's boyfriend's friend? Remember, from the Kawerak holiday party?"

"Oh yeah, I actually do remember. Isn't he kind of old?"

"I mean, Courtney's boyfriend is kind of old."

Suze and Christina looked to Lynn for an opinion, but Lynn was staring intently over Christina's shoulder. "Richard!" she called.

Suze and Christina turned to find a man bent over something large and gray sprawled out on a picnic table a few yards away from the window, focusing intently. "What is that?" Suze asked.

"Richard!"

"I think an *oogruk*," Christina said. She shouted, "Hey, Richard!"

"Who's that?" Richard looked up. He stepped away from the table, revealing the body of a half-skinned bearded seal.

"*Aapa*! Over here!" Christina waved out the window.

"Oh hey, Christy! Lynn!" Richard waved a bloody, rubber-gloved hand back. His silver hair was tied back by a red bandana, and he was sweating in the harsh sunlight despite the chill. "C'mere for a second!"

Christina shoved the rest of her fry bread into her mouth. "You guys ever seen an *oogruk*?"

"How do you even know him?" Suze muttered to Lynn.

"He's Brandon's uncle or something." Lynn pulled her coat off the back of her chair.

"Yup," Christina said. "When you guys have kids, I'm gonna be their auntie."

Suze frowned and stepped into her rubber boots. "What does *oogruk* mean?" she asked Christina.

"Bearded seal," Christina said. "Like a seal but heavier. And with more whiskers. C'mon, you've been here for almost a year."

The three women shuffled down the stairs of Christina's apartment complex and rounded the corner where Richard was working. "Hi Richard!" Lynn sang, and Richard gave her a small smile and beckoned her over.

The body of the *oogruk* lay on its side across the entire length of the picnic table. Richard had peeled a large portion of the seal's gray, furry skin away to reveal its fleshy blubber and red organs. The bearded seal's head and flippers stuck out from a bucket on the picnic bench, covered in blood. Suze squatted to look at the bearded seal's crimson face. The head was perfectly intact and the *oogruk* looked peaceful, like it was smiling. "I bet you could make fifty pairs of earrings with these whiskers," she said.

"Maybe you have learned something this year," Christina teased.

Suze stood up. "I'm Suze," she said, extending her hand to Richard. Richard held up his bloody gloves with a helpless expression, making Suze laugh. Lynn took a picture of the *oogruk* with her phone.

"Richard here makes the best *agutak* in Western Alaska," Christina told Suze. "He trades for caribou fat and I pick the berries for it and it is delicious. We tried to get the recipe from him, but I swear he leaves a secret ingredient out every time he tells it."

"Well, now." Richard looked down at his knife, and a piece of gray hair fell out of the bandana and stuck to the sweat on his chin. "I learned it from your grandmother," he told Christina. Christina shook her head at him but looked pleased. "Anyway, Christy, once I got done processing this *oogruk,* I was gonna give you the skin here to make those *mukluks* you been talkin' about. Kind of a late graduation present. Didn't think you'd be home on a beautiful day like this, so I didn't figure you'd see me out here. Your mom said you were at camp."

"Gee, thanks!" Christina beamed. "Molly's teaching me how to skin stitch, so I can probably finish a pair before winter."

Richard gave Christina a sad half-smile. "Can't believe you didn't know how to skin stitch before now. Shame on us." He glanced over the picnic table at Suze, who had gone back to examining the bucket of *oogruk* parts. "Maybe Christy here can show you how she's gonna make those *mukluks*," Richard said. "Or dry it up for blackmeat, huh. You're too skinny."

Suze stood up and glanced at Christina. "I'm probably not going to be in town by the time she starts the *mukluks*," she said.

"Well, guess you should stick around, then," said Richard. "Whatever you were gonna do down there, you can do up here."

"I'll think about it."

"Well!" Lynn said. "I'm freezing. I gotta get back inside, Richard."

"Brandon'll have to teach you to keep warm," Richard said. "Weather's just weather. Anyway, it's the time of year everyone gets sick, thinking it's warm enough to go outside without a coat. Better get back in. Christy, I'll call your mom."

"Thanks again, Richard. See you soon!" Christina led her friends back to her apartment.

"That was cool," Lynn said once they were seated around the fry bread and chili again. "The blood was so dark and red and stuck to the skin in such a vivid way, like it had been turned inside out. It was just so raw! I've never —"

"I know!" Suze cut her off. "Can you send me that picture? I want to show everyone back home."

"People at home like Brian?" Lynn asked.

"I don't know what you're talking about," Suze said. "And actually, though, I don't think a lot of people would like that. The head in the bucket. It's like, kind of graphic."

"Well, this is a good chance to educate them, right?" Lynn reached for another piece of fry bread. "It's so beautiful that he's out there on the ocean with the ice and the waves still hunting *oogruk*, you know?"

"Yeah, but I hate getting into it with people who don't know anything about Alaska," Suze said. "I'll have to think about it. Maybe I'll do it once I'm back in Connecticut or something."

"Don't leave!" Christina implored.

"I know, I know," Suze said. "But I have to graduate. And seriously, the winter was really hard for me. I got seasonal affective disorder so bad. Lynn, I don't know if you could tell, but I was so depressed. I don't think I could do it again."

"Come on, it gets better. Lynn's staying."

"She's got Brandon, though, and he's got a house. Lynn always has the best luck." Suze grinned at Lynn, who blushed.

Christina changed the subject. "Hey, Suze, when's Nick coming?"

"Um." Suze glanced out the window at the white pickup truck that had just pulled over to the side of the road. "I think now."

Her phone buzzed. She checked the screen and said, "Yep. Right now."

"How does he feel about Native hunting laws?" Lynn asked, nodding to the window.

"I have no idea."

"Well, let's get out there before he starts trying to put Richard on the radio." Christina and Suze stepped back into their boots and grabbed their windbreakers.

"I'll just clean up and let myself out," Lynn said.

"Psh, leave it," Christina called over her shoulder. "Say hi to Brandon!"

Suze waved at Richard and skipped up to the pickup. "Hey!" she called. The truck door unlocked, and Suze opened it to greet Nick. "Hey, my friend Christina's coming too. I think you guys met at the Kawerak Christmas party? Is that okay?"

"Sure thing," Nick said as Christina caught up to them. He pulled the zipper of his sweater up and down a couple of times. The girls glanced at each other. "Uh, I brought extra Vitamin Waters and granola bars, just in case. Thought you might need them. Nice to meet you again," he nodded at Christina.

Before Christina could say anything, Suze climbed into the passenger seat. "That's so sweet!" she enthused. Nick beamed at her. Christina looked between them, sighed, and pulled herself up into the back seat.

"Is that guy skinning a seal?" Nick asked Suze as he pulled off the shoulder.

"Yeah, how neat is that? I guess that's Christina's uncle?"

"Mom's cousin," Christina said from the back of the truck.

"I thought the ice went out too fast to hunt this year," Nick said.

Christina leaned forward and stuck her head between Nick and Suze's seats. "Right. They only had like a day to go out," she said. "It was pretty hard, the worst we've seen in a while. Thank God Kawerak gives us subsistence days, or Richard probably wouldn't have gotten anything. Salmon runs are supposed to be bad this year too."

Nick nodded. "That's what I heard. He's at Kawerak too? Nice."

"Yep. And you're at KNOM?"

"Yeah, I was in the army for a little bit before school, but I've been here since I graduated from college."

They passed the old Alaska Trading Company building, and Nick pressed on the gas as they drove onto the Nome-Council Road. The sun broke through the clouds, and the tundra glowed yellow against the dark backdrop of the cape. They passed the turnoff to the Kougarok Road and kept going toward Solomon. The Solomon River angled in on their left, so that they were driving between the deep blue Bering Sea and the golden river. A flock of pink cranes took off from the run of tall grass next to the riverbank, their wings glinting in the light.

Christina cleared her throat. "Did you — were you overseas?"

"Oh, yeah." Nick glanced at Christina's face in the rearview mirror. "Don't worry, I don't mind. It was actually okay — the people were pretty friendly to me. Want a water?" He handed an orange Vitamin Water back to Christina and a purple bottle over to Suze.

"Thanks, Nick."

"Yeah, so. But I really like it up here. I think I'm gonna try to get a piece of property from Sitnasuak, work on a cabin, you know. Big wraparound porch. Might not be practical though." He tapped his hands on the steering wheel.

"Nice! We're about to pass my new camp," Christina said. "This is the first summer I can actually use it. I'm so excited!"

"That's great. Nice tattoo, by the way. Haven't seen a lot of those around."

Christina touched the blue lines that ran from her lower lip to the bottom of her chin. "Thanks! It's traditional for Inupiaq women. I got it when I graduated from high school."

"Hold up!" Suze said suddenly. "Wait, stop the car." Nick checked that there was no one behind them, then stepped on the brake without pulling over to the shoulder. Suze pointed out the driver window. A shaggy brown bear and her cub perked their ears up and stared at the vehicle. Suze, Nick, and Christina stared back before Nick broke the trance and revved the engine.

"Gee, pretty close to town," Christina sighed from the backseat. "Wait, Suze, have you ever seen a bear?"

"No! I think Brian did, though."

"Brian's your roommate, right?" Nick asked.

"He was," Suze said. "We're a rotating group. He was only here for a few months. I'm going to have been here for a full year by the end of the summer."

Nick glanced at Christina in the rearview mirror. "You don't live with them?"

"Nope," Christina said. "That was my apartment you picked us up at. I'm at Kawerak. Children and Family Services."

"You must've taken my buddy's job," Nick said. "Dave? Surprised I've never run into you before." He shook his head and drummed his fingers on the steering wheel. "Are you doing that summer camp at the hospital this year?" he asked Suze.

"Yeah! It starts next week. That's my last project before I leave."

"What is this song, anyway?" Christina called from the back seat. Nick turned up KNOM and started singing along in a deep, rockabilly Elvis impression.

"So random!" Christina giggled. Nick grinned lopsidedly at her in the mirror. "Oh wait, here's my camp! I'll have to take you guys here soon!"

"That'd be so cool!" Suze said. She strained out the window to catch a glimpse of the light blue cabin as Nick drove by.

They rounded Cape Nome and continued down the dirt highway. The early summer sun was warm on their faces through the windshield. Suze put on her sunglasses.

Nick turned the radio down. "You ever been here?" he asked Suze when they passed Safety Roadhouse.

"No, not yet." Suze was surprised to see that the last stop on the Iditarod trail looked like a small barn.

"They have killer Bloody Mary's. We'll stop on the way back."

"It's a bar?"

"Ohmygod, Suze, Nome is so fun in the summer!" Christina said. "We have the Polar Bear Plunge and a folk concert for the solstice, and then races and Native games on the Fourth of July, and we can go egging and fishing and then berry picking later. You can come too," she told Nick, who smiled back tentatively.

"And the raft race," he said.

"Oh yeah, the raft race. We usually just sit on the side of the river and throw water balloons at everybody," Christina grinned. "Hey, actually I remember you doing it from last year! You and Dave looked really serious and then those girls pushed you off your raft."

"Egging?" Suze asked.

"Yeah, some birds lay their eggs on the beach, and they're so good! We go and pick them and have the best breakfasts. I'm going to take Rose's kids tomorrow. You wanna come?"

"Sure! Do you think that'd be a good thing to do with the summer camp?"

"Oh, um." Christina was quiet for a moment. "I don't

think that would be good. That would be too many people. I'm not even sure you're allowed to pick eggs if you're not Native or what. And we gotta leave some eggs to actually hatch!"

"Right, right, got it." Suze sighed and pulled down her hair. "Like, how am I supposed to come up with stuff for the kids to do?"

"Ah, don't worry about it. You've got me." Christina reached around the passenger seat and shook Suze's shoulders lightly until Suze giggled.

"Thanks, Christina," she said.

When the river turned north, Nick followed it away from the Bering Sea and into the foothills. The sun graced the tundra and small tributaries with glittering light as the truck passed an abandoned dredge and some overgrown fishing banks. Christina and Suze leaned out the windows whenever they passed a trail, but Nick pressed onward into the foothills. "I just want some sunlight to see this thing," he said. "If you guys want to check out any of this stuff on the way back, we can do that. There's a nice fishing spot we can sit at too, if you don't want to go to Safety."

Suze was leaning out the window to let the sunlight play with her red hair. "How often do you get out here?" she asked.

"As often as I can in the summer. Because I don't have the cabin yet, this is the closest I can get to camp. I just — I can't believe I'd never seen this cave before last week. Makes me feel like I haven't been paying attention or something." The tundra on either side of the truck rose into the mountains. The peaks were lined with silver in the evening sun. "It should be right here, between Mile Thirty-Four and Thirty-Five." Nick slowed down, scanning the ridges to the left of the truck.

They drove past the Mile Thirty-Six marker without seeing the cave, and Nick did a U-Turn. He took his hat off and put it back on twice. "I swear it was here," he said.

"I see it!" Christina called from the back.

"Where at?"

"Right up there." Christina leaned forward and pointed toward the cliff on the left. A small, round opening in the rock was just visible under the rays of the sun.

"Woah, that's way higher than it looked from the chopper," Nick said. "I don't know if we're going to be able to get up there. Let's check it out."

Nick pulled over to the side of the road. Suze tugged at her rain boots as Christina put on her windbreaker in the back seat. Nick leaned over, popped the glove compartment, and took out a heavy sidearm. "Um," Suze stammered.

"For the bears," Nick explained. "This probably wouldn't do much, though. It's mostly for my own peace of mind."

"You ever shot a gun?" Christina asked Suze.

"Yeah, Dave took us out to shoot bottles by the side of the Teller Road over the winter," Suze said. "Brian didn't hit a single bottle but did get a ptarmigan by accident."

Nick smiled and tapped the stock of his sidearm three times. "Dave probably hated that."

The cliff was further from the road than it had appeared from the car. Tall green willows sprung up from the tundra ahead of the rock face, creating a thicket in the otherwise barren landscape. "Probably a creek here," Nick said. "I'll go ahead."

"Bears bears bears," Suze sang, as she and Christina followed behind Nick. "Bears bears bears!" Christina laughed. "What? I'm making noise to keep them away!"

As Nick predicted, the tundra sloped down into a shallow brook, and the trio waded across to reach the base of the cliff face. Clear, cool water lapped at their boots as they peered up at the entrance to the cave. The rock face was steeply vertical, but uneven, with rocks jutting out of the cliff. The sun had already journeyed to the other side of the ridge, rendering the cave almost invisible against the dark rock. Christina put her hand on the cliff. "I guess we could climb this," she said.

"I could hoist you ladies up," Nick offered. "I don't think I'm gonna be able to make it." He gazed sadly at his boots. "I think if I were maybe back in army shape."

"Well, let's just try. Maybe we can pull you up or something," Suze said brightly. She caught Christina's eye as Nick smiled softly. "What?" she said. "I can go first."

"I hope there's nothing in there," Nick mused.

"Bats?" Christina asked, shielding her eyes to get a better look at the cave.

Nick chuckled. "A bear?"

"Too small for a bear," Christina admonished.

"Everybody got their rabies shot?" Suze put her foot on the base of the incline, causing several rocks to tumble down into the stream.

"Yeah, right," Nick said.

"Where do you even get those?"

"Okay, well, we didn't drive out here for nothing," Suze said. She grabbed lightly at the rock face to find a solid handhold.

"Here." Nick moved next to Suze and cupped his hands together. "You can step here, don't worry. You weigh like a hundred pounds."

Suze looked unsure for only a second before pulling her boot out of the stream and putting her sole in Nick's extended palms. She leaned on his shoulder as he lifted her up, then twisted away from him and grabbed one of the rocks that jutted out from the slope. She clung to the cliff face for a moment, then scrambled up the ledge. Her climb brought her right to the mouth of the cave. "Hello?" she whispered into the darkness. When nothing moved in the cavern, she called more loudly, "Hello?" Still quiet. Suze stuck her head back over the ridge. Nick shielded his eyes while Christina waved at her. "Come on, Christina!" she yelled. "You can get up here."

"Do you mind?" Christina asked Nick. He offered her his cupped palms. Christina gingerly placed her boot on the edge of his fingertips, then leapt from his hands, gripped the rock face, and hauled herself up into the cave until she was seated next to Suze.

"I don't think I'm gonna make it!" Nick shouted from below.

"We'll take pictures for you!" Suze assured him.

"I'll keep a lookout for bears!"

Suze smiled and turned back toward the cave. "He's nice," Christina whispered to her. Then, more loudly, "Oh man, this is so shallow. What a letdown."

The top of the cave reached Suze's forehead and stood two inches above Christina's high ponytail as the women knelt at the entrance. Both women ducked forward to get a better look inside. Suze used her cell phone to illuminate the cavern, but the back wall of the cave caught the light after only three feet. Suze sighed. "You're not missing anything!" she called down to Nick.

"Wait, I see something." Christina edged forward on her knees and reached toward the right wall. "Here!" she said triumphantly, and handed a heavy, rusted, green metal box back to Suze.

"Woah," Suze marveled. "How old do you think this is?"

"Dunno," Christina said. "Let's open it."

"Maybe it's a gold miner's kit or something from when they were building the railroad? That'd make it like, super old."

Both women sat back on their heels as Suze cautiously pulled the lid open to reveal a dirty Ziploc bag full of trinkets.

"Aw shit, it's just a geocache," Christina said.

"What's a geocache?" Suze asked as she pried the Ziploc open.

"It's like, I guess a thing that hipsters do when they travel. You hide stuff somewhere and can post the coordinates of the thing you leave online, and other people go on the website or app or whatever and try to find it. There are lots of these in Nome. It looks like a bunch of people have been here already." Christina wrinkled her nose at the collection of bobby pins, Sacajawea dollars, and empty bullet casings. "Ew."

"Hey, look," Suze flipped open a small notebook she had extracted from the plastic bag. "This is everybody who's been here."

Christina peered over her shoulder. "It only goes back to 2011. Bummer. Ugh, everyone who writes in this is from out of town, too. They were probably all here for like, not even a year. No offense. I literally do not see anyone from Western Alaska in here."

Suze shrugged and put the notebook down, then leaned away from the mouth of the cave. Nick was pacing at the foot of the cliff, running his hands over the rocks. "Hey!" she yelled down the ridge, making him jump. "There's a geocache up here. Do you want to leave anything?"

"Give me a second!" Nick abandoned his post and sloshed through the stream to his truck. Suze watched him pull something out of the glove compartment before heading back to the cave. "Here," he said, throwing something upward. Suze reached down to catch his memento. It was a crisp, black army patch.

"What're you gonna add?" Christina asked Suze.

"I don't have anything with me. I think I'm just going to write my name in the book."

"The patch can be yours too," Nick offered from below. "You're the one actually up there. Just write my name in the book with yours. You too, Christina, if you want."

Christina raised her eyebrows at Suze and started digging through the pockets of her windbreaker.

"What're you looking for?" Suze asked.

"Found it!" Christina held up a small earring carved in the shape of an *ulu*. The walrus ivory was bright in the dark cavern. "I've been carrying this around with me in case I found the other one. I haven't found it, so I'll leave it. There isn't any Native stuff in here at all, and I mean, if I'm going to be the first Inupiaq to put anything in this box, I wanna represent. Just to remind everybody that we actually live here." She ran her finger over the *ulu*'s miniature blade and placed the earring gently in the plastic bag. "There. We were here first, and don't you forget it."

Christina handed the box back to Suze, who added the army patch and sealed the Ziploc. She set the box back into the maw of the cave and stretched her legs out next to it. The women sat in silence, listening to the wind sweep through the mountains.

"Guys?" Nick called. "It's getting kind of late. I want to show you my fishing spot."

"Coming!" Christina used Suze's shoulder to pull herself to her feet. She leaned over the edge of the cliff to determine the best descent strategy, then climbed back down the jagged rock face feet-first and landed in the stream without accepting Nick's outstretched hand.

Suze looked back at the geocache, then tested a groove below the cave with her boot before putting her full weight on the slope. A piece of rock broke off and Suze pulled back quickly. She looked for a different route. Nick kept his hand in the air to offer her help, but he had turned toward Christina.

Christina stood in the river with her hands on her hips, smiling at Nick. "Hey, you should come fish with me sometime," Nick was saying. "I've got a new boat we could go out on. We could go out from your camp, or, you know, if you're not comfortable with that, we could just go out from the beach."

"Yeah," Christina said to Nick. "Let's go fishing. We have a boat too. You can come to camp any time. That would be great."

Suze perched on the ledge for a moment longer, watching them, then quietly slid down the rock face on her own.

❄ ❄ ❄

fatherhood

ETHAN CLOSED ONE EYE AND FOCUSED ON the first step of his front porch. He placed his right heel directly in front of the toe of his left boot and rocked back and forth, feeling the solid ground beneath his feet. Brenda, his laughing little girl, tried to toddle past him to the four wheeler, but he caught her against his knee with one eye still closed. Ethan's pre-driving ritual served to combat his lingering fear that he had lost some of his vision when he had gone snow-blind last winter on the North Slope. He'd had his eyes checked at the new hospital, but he didn't really trust the doctors there, and he felt slower than he had before, as if the sun had burnt not just his eyes but his brain as well. But they needed to get going. His shifts on the Slope took him hundreds of miles away from his family for long stretches, so his time with his baby girl was precious. He had so much to teach her, and to teach her he needed to be out of town and on the land with her. The ritual also reminded him to be careful when he drove with her, to make sure he was fully present for each ride and that his reflexes were quick.

Brenda ducked out from under his hand. Ethan noticed sadly that the folds of baby fat in her legs were disappearing. He used to take Brenda for long rides on his four wheeler when she was just a pudgy baby strapped to his back. "For eggs!" she now said proudly, handing an egg carton up to Ethan.

"Very good," he said, taking the carton from her. "Let's try to fill this up maybe halfway today. We can get some for your mom and all have them for breakfast tomorrow. Good plan?"

"Yeah!"

"Good. Now get on up there."

"Can I sit on the back?" she asked.

"Well, now," Ethan said. He glanced at his wife, who was watching them from the doorway of their house. She shook her head, barely, so Brenda wouldn't see. "I don't think you're quite old enough yet, baby girl."

"Daddy!" Brenda whined. She scrunched up her face to threaten a tantrum.

"You only call me daddy when you want something," Ethan said gently. Brenda immediately unscrunched her face to plead up at him with her big pup eyes. He handed the egg carton back to her. "Go on, put this in the back and then get up on the seat with me."

Brenda stored the carton in the back of the ATV and scrambled onto the front seat of the four wheeler. Ethan secured her lime green helmet, and she shook her head from side to side to make sure it didn't budge. "Dad, what about your helmet?"

"Good idea, baby girl." Ethan looped the strap of his own helmet under his chin. "Always wear a helmet."

Ethan waved to his wife as he pulled out of their yard. Brenda held onto the steering column with both hands, bracing herself against the turn as Ethan merged onto their street. She let her head fall dramatically forward with each stop sign as the ATV jogged through town, but Ethan ignored her; he didn't reward bad behavior with attention, and she stopped goofing around by the fourth intersection as they headed out of Nome. The streets were in bad shape: winter had ended, but the construction sites were not yet in place to repair the unpaved roads. They couldn't go as quickly as Brenda wanted until they hit the highway.

"Ready?" Ethan asked when they reached the edge of town, where Front Street turned into the Nome-Council Road.

"Ready!" Brenda screamed.

Ethan revved the engine and stepped on the gas, pushing the ATV not nearly as fast as it could go but giving it more speed than he had in town. Brenda's fingers were turning red and white on the steering column as Ethan drove, so Ethan flexed his thighs together to give her some extra security on the vehicle. He couldn't hear her over the engine, but he knew she was yelling, tasting the air and sand with her tongue. He couldn't fathom how his daughter was growing up to be so damn loud.

The rocky sea wall fell away as they drove further up the coast, and green patches of tundra sprung up along both sides of the road. Ethan chanted in Brenda's ear to quiet her. "*Tukaiyuk, atchaaqluk, kimagluk, asiavik,*" he sang, raising his voice against the wind to name every plant he could remember from his own home in Barrow and the words his wife had taught him. Brenda stopped yelling to listen to him. "Should we pick some greens for Mom before we go egging?" Ethan asked.

"Yeah!"

"Let's get a little further out, baby girl." The four wheeler rumbled onward, past the turnoff. The beach was deserted on their right and the tundra empty on their left. Light gray clouds coated the sky, muting the landscape and hinting at rain. Ethan was concerned that he couldn't see any variation in the cloudy skies; the sky just looked like one bright, gray sheet. Maybe that's just how it was, he thought. The mountains that lined Cape Nome rose up ahead, their silhouettes faint, but the road looked muddy and Ethan knew that Brenda wouldn't have the patience for a longer ride. His daughter was already squirming on his lap.

Ethan pulled over to the right shoulder. "This look like a good spot?" he asked the top of Brenda's head.

"Yeah!" Brenda hopped off the four wheeler, bright pink raincoat and neon helmet vibrant against the gray seascape.

"Good girl." Ethan helped Brenda take off her helmet, then took off his own. He set both helmets next to the ATV, then picked Brenda up and put her on his shoulders to carry her across the road to the tundra. He put her down on the other side of the highway and squatted to talk to her face-to-face. "Remember what I showed you last week? You can use the pocket of your hoodie, under your coat, for storing greens." Ethan leaned down and picked up some greens off the tundra and put them in the stomach pocket of his own black hoodie. "See? *Tukaiyuk*. It grows by the beach."

Brenda nodded. She bent down and grabbed a handful of tundra to show Ethan. The green, red, and white plants crumbled through her fingers.

"Ah, baby girl, you've got to look at what you're picking. We want to make *niqipiaq*, Native food, see. We can't just eat anything. See these?" He picked a green plant out of the soil and held it up for Brenda. "It's the size of your thumb, see? *Atchaaqluk*. Beach greens. We can eat these too. We don't want to eat dirt, do we? That's yucky."

"Yucky," Brenda repeated, sticking out her tongue.

"That's right. We pick these." He held out the tiny plant again. "Can you show me which ones we pick?"

Brenda reached down to her feet and pulled up a *tukaiyuk* stem, its little green head drooping in her pudgy fist. "Here, Dad. *Tukaiyuk*," she offered.

Ethan felt his chest expand with pride. He had never loved anyone so much as he loved this little girl. "That's right. *Tukaiyuk*. You and me and Mom, our people have been picking *tukaiyuks* since we got here. Your grandmas pick it, your great grandmas picked it, and even their grandmas picked it. When we pick, we remember them, see, and remember that we live on the land. Plus if you eat these, especially if you have them set in seal oil, you'll grow up strong and beat everybody in the Native games."

"What's that?"

"You remember watching those girls compete down in Anchorage?"

Brenda shook her head.

"Ah, okay. Well, see, when you were real little we watched lots of girls and boys do Native games in a gym in Anchorage. It's called the Native Youth Olympics. And they're games, so they're fun, but they're also about hunting and survival. Our way is hard sometimes, right? You can be out there, on the ice, hunting seal, and suddenly the ice starts to break up." Brenda watched Ethan intensely, *tukaiyuk* clutched, forgotten, in her hand. "And when the ice breaks up, see, you have to be able to get back to shore, or get on the biggest floating chunk of ice so you don't sink. If you're standing on a little chunk of ice, see, and surrounded by little chunks of ice, you gotta move pretty quickly to make it to a bigger chunk. So you dance on the ice, like a, um, like a ballerina. Just landing enough on the ice so that you stay above the water. Then you can make it back to shore. But to do that you sure have to be strong. You have to be real quick. You have to practice. So the Native games are a way of practicing."

"Like a ballerina?" Brenda asked.

"Yes, like a ballerina. I went to Anchorage for the Olympics one time. Got pretty good on the seal hop. Now I'm too fat, though." Ethan patted the front pocket of his hoodie and Brenda giggled. "Maybe we can talk to Uncle Richard and see if you can start practicing with the big kids," Ethan said. "I bet your cousins would help you. Would you like that?"

"No." Brenda shook her head, then grinned at Ethan.

"Baby girl, quit buggin'. I'll talk to Richard. You're gonna have to call him Coach Richard if you start practicing with him, huh." Brenda was kicking at the tundra, bored. Ethan was sure she would love being on the Nome Native Youth Olympics team; they would have to talk about it again later. "Wanna help me pick some greens?"

"Yeah!"

Ethan and Brenda moved away from the side of the road so that Ethan could be sure Brenda wouldn't wander onto the highway. The tundra was just starting to fill out, so it was easy to spot the greens on the land. Ethan made sure to keep Brenda in his field of vision. He was glad that she was dressed in such bright colors. She bent at the waist to pick each plant and put it carefully in the pocket of her hoodie, humming a high, tuneless hum. A car passed them occasionally, and if Ethan knew the driver, he waved.

When Brenda's humming reached a certain note, a note that in her infancy signaled a tantrum, Ethan knew that it was time to do something else. "Hey, baby girl, want some chips?"

Brenda nodded, chin quivering. Ethan felt guilty; he always forgot how much she needed to eat. He pulled a bag of Doritos out of his backpack. Brenda sat down on the tundra, and Ethan sat next to her to eat the orange chips in the gray light.

After a while, Ethan said, "How about we go to the beach and try to find some eggs for Mom?"

"Can we go home?" Brenda asked.

"Not yet, not yet. We're spending the day together, see. In the winter you can stay home as much as you want, but during the summer we've got to work. You can keep some of the stuff we get, like the greens, over the winter so you and Mom can have vegetables and good food. You're a big girl now, so I'm teaching you how to help. I won't be here much in the winter, remember, so you're going to have to help Mom."

"Okay." Brenda sprawled out dramatically on the tundra. Ethan noticed she was scratching at a mosquito bite on her cheek. He was glad that he'd cut her fingernails yesterday.

"Hey, get up. You're going to get all wet." Ethan put a hand under Brenda's padded shoulders and helped her sit up. "Let's go get some eggs."

Ethan stood and walked to the road. Brenda scampered up behind him, so he held his arms out to stop her from careening onto the highway. He exaggeratedly checked for cars in both directions to demonstrate road safety. There wasn't another vehicle in sight. He held out his hand and Brenda took it, and together they crossed the dirt-packed road.

"Dad!" Brenda yelled. "Egg carton!"

"Smart, baby girl!" Ethan said. He took the egg carton out of the four wheeler's storage and put it under his arm. Brenda almost tripped as they slid down the embankment toward the beach, but Ethan held her hand firmly as she toddled over the small dunes toward the shore.

"Now, you gotta keep your eyes on the sand here," Ethan said. "That's where the birds build their nests." He started moving slowly toward the cape, waiting for Brenda to catch up every few steps. Father and daughter scanned the ground, looking for mottled blue eggs.

"What's that?" Brenda asked. Ethan looked down and saw that his daughter was pointing ahead of them toward the cape. Ethan squinted. A white bird, the size of a sleek and angular seagull, was hovering twenty feet off the ground in front of them. Ethan could barely see it against the cloudy sky. A black cap of feathers covered its head and came down to the top of its sharp red beak.

"That's a tern, baby girl. *Mit* — ah, I can't remember what we call it. I'll tell you later. But see, white wings and that black *niaquq*." Ethan tapped Brenda on the top of her head and she giggled. "That's a mom or dad tern. Both parents watch their babies, just like us," he said. "Maybe that's a mom tern, and the dad's out working, like how I go to the North Slope in the winter. There must be a nest right there. They've got pretty good eggs, and when they see someone coming, they fly up in the air right over the nest so that people don't try to pick them. C'mere for a minute." Brenda waddled over to Ethan. "Do you want to come with me to get the eggs?"

Brenda nodded.

"Very good," he said. "Here's my sweatshirt." He set his backpack down and pulled off his hoodie. "You have to hold it over your head, okay? Terns protect their nests, and they dive bomb you like this if you get too close." Ethan made a beak with his fingers and pecked at the top of Brenda's head. "Hold my coat up so it doesn't get to your eyes or anything, okay?"

"What about you, Dad?" Brenda asked.

"Well, see, I'm a grown-up, so I can just use my arms. And if the tern comes down too strong, just back up. They'll let you go if you're not near their eggs. They're not going to attack you for nothing. They're just trying to protect their nests. So if the tern's going after you, or if the dad bird joins it, just wait for me right back here."

"Okay." Brenda covered her head with Ethan's hoodie, pulling it low over her face. Ethan took her hand, and they started inching forward. Ethan saw the nest, four green-gray eggs resting in a hollow in the sand. "See the nest right there?"

Brenda shook her head.

"Okay, let's move a little closer then." Ethan took a larger step forward, and Brenda took two to keep up. The tern cried a piercing cry but stayed in place. "Ready?" Ethan asked.

"Ready," Brenda said.

Ethan took another exaggerated lunge. Brenda giggled. The tern called again, its agitated wings losing the rhythm of the air currents. Its black head twitched compulsively. Ethan tried to keep an eye on it but couldn't make out the rest of the bird's body against the light gray backdrop.

"Eggs!" Brenda called beside him, catching sight of the dip in the sand that led to the tern's nest. The black hoodie had slipped down over her shoulders, revealing her black hair and shining, excited eyes. Ethan smiled. She looked exactly like her grandmother.

"That's right!" Ethan glanced at the nest, only a few feet in front of them. "Let's go get 'em!" He gave Brenda's hand a squeeze and let it go. She would need both hands to grab an egg without breaking it.

When he looked back to the sky, the tern had disappeared. At first, Ethan thought it was his eyes and strained to see the bird's black head bobbing against the clouds. He realized too late that the tern had flown higher to gain the offensive, and he threw his arms over his head to ward off the oncoming attack. Silence. Ethan put his arms down and scanned the bright gray horizon, knowing what would come next but unable to move quickly enough, to even see the bird, to stop the next scene from unfolding. He crouched helplessly within reach of the stormy green eggs.

Then Brenda screamed. Her wail seemed to come from a body much larger than hers, and the cry echoed off the cape so that Ethan felt his daughter had suddenly multiplied until she was standing on all sides of him hollering at his face, his ears, and his back. Through the scream, Ethan heard the shrill punctures of the tern. He turned to face the noise and saw his daughter, small and earthbound, crouching and covering her face while the red-beaked bird dove at her from the sky. Brenda had her eyes shut tight, right arm raised above her head and the other clenching the hoodie pocket that held her picked greens. Ethan couldn't seem to move. He stood, stupefied, as Brenda took her left hand off her stomach and raised it above her head. Some greens blew out from her pocket and onto the beach.

Ethan's throat unlocked as soon as the first leaf landed on the gray sand. "Hey!" he shouted at the bird. The tern darted away from him, tightening its attack on Brenda. Ethan's mouth was dry in the subarctic desert air, his voice painful and hoarse. "Hey!" he roared. "Get away! Get away!"

The tern ignored him and continued its aerial bombardment. Ethan dropped the egg carton on the beach and lunged toward the circling bird, standing above Brenda so that he could protect her head. He swatted randomly, making large half-moon arcs across his face, not trying to hit the bird but to wave it away. It was the most persistent tern he had ever encountered. The bird retreated slightly, pumping its wings, and Ethan lost sight of the vague outline of its body against the sky. Brenda whimpered between Ethan's legs, and Ethan made a final crescent with his arm, just enough to create a protective circle around his child against the now-invisible bird. If he and

Brenda could get just a few feet further from the nest they would be safe. The tern would not venture too far. Even as he made these calculations, though, the bird's black head materialized to their right, and the back of Ethan's hand collided with the tern's invisible white belly. Ethan felt the brittle bones of the bird against the stand-out veins on the back of his fingers as the tern resisted, then gave into, the force of the impact. The tern sprawled on the sand, its wing bent starkly outward. Ethan covered Brenda's eyes as the bird twitched.

The beach was quiet again but for the wind and Ethan's heavy breathing. Brenda clung to Ethan's leg, round flushed face planted into his right thigh. Ethan put his hand on her shoulder. Her tiny body shuddered, and she let out a few whimpering cries.

The nest lay abandoned just a few yards away. "Hey," Ethan said. He pulled Brenda gently away from his leg and squatted down to look at her. Her eyes were swollen from crying, and a trail of snot was drying under her nose, but she looked uninjured. He picked his hoodie up off the beach and used a clean section of it to wipe her face. "Want to get those eggs for Mom?" he asked. Brenda looked at him with an expression of great betrayal. Ethan faltered for a moment, but put his hand on Brenda's shoulder to reassure her. He didn't want her to be afraid of any part of subsistence. He wanted her to have a long, productive, nutritious relationship with the land, cautious and prepared, but not fearful. "C'mon, we're not going to let that bird push us around, right? We're brave."

Brenda sniffed and tentatively took Ethan's outstretched hand. The pair walked slowly toward the nest, shuffling their sneakered feet over the damp sand. Ethan scanned the horizon for another black feathered head and red beak as Brenda looked up worriedly, but the clouds seemed empty. "Okay, go get one," Ethan said, letting go of Brenda's hand. He gave her a light pat on the back, and she ran up to the nest, grabbed one of the gray-green eggs with both hands, and waddled back to him triumphantly. "What a helper!" Ethan smiled as Brenda offered him the egg. "Thank you!" He put the egg in the carton and ruffled her hair affectionately.

A white wing flashed in the corner of Ethan's vision. He didn't turn to see if it was real or if his eyes were tricking him, but picked Brenda up and threw her over his shoulder. "Let's race!" Ethan shouted above the wind as he started to trot toward the four wheeler.

"Race!" Brenda shouted. Ethan was proud that she was giggling, already recovering, as he ran to the vehicle. Brenda didn't see the red-beaked bird, the fallen tern's mate, that followed them, flapping hard against the wind, before returning to its nest to keep watch over the rest of its eggs. Brenda opened her mouth and yelled joyfully, interrupting herself with each bounce of Ethan's shoulder, but making sure to hold her hand over the pocket of her hoodie to keep the rest of her greens safe.

❈ ❈ ❈

uqsruq

MOLLY'S EYES FLUTTERED OPEN IN THE
darkness. For a moment she lay still and
listened to the scratch scratch scratching of what sounded like an infantry
of mice clawing through the walls of
her bedroom, daring herself to face
the commotion. She breathed deeply
into the warm musk of her blankets. It
was winter. She hadn't slept through a
winter night in forty-two years.

The scratching became more
urgent, and Molly felt her heart pound
faster in her chest. Although she had
listened to this ritual thousands of
times, she could not ward off the
innate panic that gripped her whenever she heard the anguished scraping
sounds. Molly caught her breath and
slowed it, then extracted her arm from
under her pile of blankets. Each inch
of skin froze as it left the soft cocoon

of her bed. Once her arm was free, Molly extended her hand toward the furious scuffle and laid it on her husband's scabbed shoulder.

The scratching stopped. Molly's husband jerked not-quite awake and grabbed her hand. She could feel warm blood on her husband's fingernails and shoulder where he had scratched through his cracked, wrecked skin. She would have to change the sheets in the morning.

Molly waited for her husband's breathing to even, then heaved off her pile of blankets. She slid her feet into the slippers she kept waiting next to the bed and stretched to align her shoulders and back. The night exploded into a thousand green sparklers before her eyes, and she waited for her vision to clear before she stood. Without turning on the light, Molly gathered the topmost blanket around her shoulders and shuffled out of the bedroom.

Molly took a wide berth through the living room to avoid waking her youngest grandson, who was sleeping under his own nest of blankets on the couch. A street light glowed through the small window over the sink, giving Molly enough light to find the handle of the refrigerator. Straining from the shoulder, Molly pulled the refrigerator open and peered at the nearly-empty shelves inside.

Her jar of *uqsruq*, oil made from seal blubber, was all the way in the back of the fridge. It had turned a deep yellow, and Molly knew that if she opened it here, the pungent smell would wake her grandson in a moment. Molly sighed; most of her grandchildren didn't like to come over to their house because the smell of seal oil clung to the blankets, furniture, and clothing, and took some getting used to. They'd never taught their children to make *niqipiaq*, hadn't realize it was something that they would have to teach, really, and then their grandkids didn't smell seal oil until they were older and they weren't accustomed to it. Their oldest grandchild had begun to appreciate its value, though: he had joined a dance group and sprayed seal oil on his drum keep the gut firm. She hoped that he would come to love it, to begin to use the oil to store greens and dip his fish and soothe the eczema-ridden skin he had inherited from his grandfather. Maybe then she would be able to turn to her grandchildren when she needed seal oil instead of relying on the generosity of other families in town.

Molly felt the sting of an ancient frost nip injury in the tips of her fingers as she grabbed the jar. She stood quickly and let the sparks that flooded her vision dissipate before closing the fridge and shuffling back to the bedroom. Her grandson slept as if dead under the weight of his blanket fortress.

Molly could hear scratching as soon as she entered the bedroom. She dipped two fingers into the thick yellow oil, cupping her hand so that none would fall, and reached out to the dark mound that she knew was her husband's bare shoulder. Molly rubbed the seal oil onto his chapped flesh, careful to avoid his scratching fingers. She hadn't used enough oil to ease the itching yet, but her husband stopped scratching and sighed in relief at the familiar smell.

Making small circles with her hand, Molly gently kneaded the oil into her husband's exposed shoulder blade. She used as little as she could to cover the rest of his arm and neck, feeling for scabs and wounds in the darkness. In the morning, she would have just a glimpse of her husband's sore-covered skin before he pulled on a sweatshirt and turned away from her.

When she had finished covering as much of her husband's torso as she could in seal oil, Molly tightened the lid of the jar and put it on the floor. The house was cold enough to keep the oil until morning. She crawled under her pile of blankets and listened to her husband's peaceful breathing on the other side of the bed. Molly turned her face toward the ceiling, raised the top blanket to the tip of her nose, and fell into a dreamless sleep.

acknowledgments

THANK YOU TO EVERYONE WHO INVITED ME INTO THEIR HOMES and hearts during the year I lived in Nome. I was so lucky to work, learn, and explore in such a unique community with such wonderful people. Thank you also to everyone who read and commented on the original manuscript; writing has a reputation for being a solitary activity, but this project was definitely a group effort and much richer for it. Finally, thank you to my parents, who have been unendingly supportive of all my many dreams.

The Inupiaq story in "Taboo" is based on "The Kiligvak Hunter: A Story from Anaktuvuk Pass," as told by Simon Paneak and Elijah Kakinya. For more information on this story and to hear the original story in Inupiaq, please visit the Iñupiat Heritage Center in Barrow. A video of the story and surrounding context provided by the Iñupiat Heritage Center is available on School Tube, titled "OWL Videoconference: Kiligvak Hunter: A Story from Anaktuvuk Pass, January 31, 2014." The Iñupiat Heritage Center is not affiliated with any views or events expressed in *On the Great Land*.

colophon

WHEN FRANCESCO GRIFFO CUT THE ROMAN PLATES FOR A FONT in 1495, he had to wait a year before the Venitian printer Aldus Manutius used them in a travel journal about Mt. Aetna by Cardinal Pietro Bembo (de Aetna). They called their font Bembo. When Bembo was recut for modern printing processes at the Monotype Corporation in the late 1920s, it was found to be perfect for modern book-making. For decades monographs from the publishers Oxford, Everyman, Cambridge, and Penguin used Bembo for novels, short story collections, and even nonfiction volumes. Now in the digital age, the creation of Bembo Book reveals a face that is slightly narrower than previous versions of the font, where lowercase letters ascend visibly beyond the capitals giving an elegant, graceful look to the page. This serene face pairs perfectly with the stories in *On the Great Land*.

WARD STREET PRESS

61555526R00139

Made in the USA
Middletown, DE
12 January 2018